brendan connell

CANNIBALS OF
WEST PAPUA

THIS IS A SNUGGLY BOOK

ISBN: 978-1-64525-116-3

CANNIBALS OF WEST PAPUA

Brendan Connell was born in Santa Fe, New Mexico, in 1970. His works of fiction include *The Translation of Father Torturo* (Prime Books, 2005), *The Architect* (PS Publishing, 2012), *Lives of Notorious Cooks* (Chômu Press, 2012), *Miss Homicide Plays the Flute* (Eibonvale Press, 2013), *Against the Grain Again: The Further Adventures of Des Esseintes* (Tartarus Press, 2021), and *Heqet* (Egaeus Press, 2022). As editor he has worked on various projects, including *The World in Violet: An Anthology of English Decadent Poetry* (Snuggly Boos, 2022), and *The Neo-Decadent Cookbook* (Eibonvale Press, 2020), which was co-edited by Justin Isis. As translator his efforts include *Alcina and Other Stories* (Snuggly Books, 2019), by Guido Gozzano, which was co-translated by his wife Anna.

SNUGGLY BOOKS

To the rich and *industrious* of the world, I dedicate this book—to the members of the International Council of Mining and Metals, to the corporate executives and chairmen and seekers and holders of public office, to the Copper Man of the Year, to the economists and to those who have senior administrative positions, to the Ministers of Mining and Energy, to the army generals who become presidents, to the principal shareholders and those who process the Earth's mineral resources in order to maximise gain for their shareholders—yes, to you I dedicate these pages of blood and violence, may they stir in others the disgust you stir in me.

CANNIBALS OF WEST PAPUA

Once a sea-bird alighted in the suburban country of Lû. The marquis went out to meet it, brought it to the ancestral temple and prepared to banquet it there. The Kiû-shâo was performed to afford it music; an ox, a sheep and a pig were killed to supply the food. The bird, however, looked at everything with dim eyes, and was very sad. It did not venture to eat a single bit of flesh, nor to drink a single cupful; and in three days it died.

—Chuang Tzu, *Perfect Enjoyment*

1

"ARE we far?"
"Eh?"
"Are we far?"
"We are very near."
"Where?"
"Near. Near."
"I don't see any signs of habitation. Only forest."

"Fifteen minutes," the pilot, whose name was Manuel Sergio, said, opening and closing his left hand three times to indicate the math.

The sound of the engine made talking difficult and down below there was that vast expanse of green, deceptively beautiful, without any signs of highways, housing, or civilisation—instead a flowing sea of hypnotic violence, where snakes ate monkeys and were in turn eaten by alligators, in horrible struggles for survival out of which sprang dazzling, vulva-like orchids and strangling vines, and Dom Ramiro had to wonder why the Lord God had made such a place since he had already made hell.

This was New Guinea, one of the most remote parts of West Papua, a place of ancient and dense growth of trees, danger and a richness of life—some stunning tragedy of birth and rebirth and primeval stones and adolescent flowers. Looking below, the priest was both a little awed and a little frightened. It was impossible not to acknowledge the charm of the land—but to admire the charms of a landscape and to be thrust physically into the picture are two very different things—the impenetrable sea of beryl below, with its crests and swirling forests, was something that almost took his breath away and in him keen anticipation was somewhat choked by subdued apprehension, and he grinned and showed his teeth and crossed himself.

Manuel on the other hand seemed little impressed. A Filipino by birth, he had come to Papua some fifteen years before—hired by a mining company to transport executives by helicopter. But after five years of this, he had been let go due to excessive drinking. Now he ran a private service—doing jobs that no one else would do because they were too unsafe, in an old Bell 47 that he had taken apart and rebuilt, repaired and re-repaired countless times.

He was a muscular individual with a handsome though dissipated face, the sharp-eyes of which were shielded by a pair of mirror-lensed sunglasses. His mouth would often bend into an attractive smile, the corners sharp, slightly cruel, like some crescent-shaped blade. He flew the helicopter with great skill—with the ease of a man who knew every nut and bolt of his machine.

Soon he pointed to a little cluster of houses with smoke rising out of them and Dom Ramiro nodded his round, stubborn head and, impulsively, clutched his rosary, his mind silently reciting some prayer he had learned long ago—a plea for supernatural zeal and help in weak endeavours.

The helicopter circled once, and then landed in a little field and was immediately surrounded by half-clothed Papuans who came running up, smiles on their faces, in cheerful spirits. The pilot shut off the engine and the propellers slowed to a halt.

"Here we are," he said, "just where you told me to go. Patntrm Village."

When Dom Ramiro stepped out, the children laughed at him, at his rat like face, with its sharp nose and small, unhappy eyes. He indeed looked like one of those strange, nocturnal forest creatures that they would wrap in a giant banana leaf and roast over the fire and it was no wonder that the sight of him caused such merriment.

"A happy people," he said under his breath with disdain.

Their smiles and laughter irritated him and he glared back with ill-concealed disgust. It was clear that they were still heathens, about as Christian as dogs or wolves or crickets or worms, and that the man who had been sent to take charge of their welfare had not been up to the job. No crosses hung about their necks. They were without respect for his cassock. Their hearts had not yet been bleached by the words of the good book.

"Don't mind them," Manuel said, shoving a pistol in his belt. "They are forest people. Very ignorant people."

Dom Ramiro shrugged his shoulders. Yes, he well knew the dullness of primitives. He had recited the liturgy to Yaminahua Indians in Bolivia and baptised Kaonde babies in Zambia—for years been keen on proselytizing the primogenous, turning them from the worship of their dubious gods towards He, who is the Son of God; bury the idols, raise the standard, cleanse with myrrh—display the topaz good of the creator and ruler of the universe.

Manuel proceeded to unload the priest's bags and boxes from the machine while the latter watched a slight figure, a white woman with a white wimple over her head, dressed in a grey tunic secured around the waist by a white cloth belt from which hung a heavy wooden rosary, make her way towards them, a young Papuan by her side.

"I am Sister Justina," she said, as she stepped before him.

The Portuguese acknowledged her with a slight bow and stated his own name, as a matter of formality, as she surely already knew who he was.

She was probably not more than thirty years of age. Her face was oval, her figure slight, and her eyes were intelligent and kind. She was not beautiful—looked like a woman who had suffered—as was befitting for one who had taken up God's cause and left the hopes of the world behind—but her features had a warmth of expression that lent her face an attractive quality that many much more handsome women certainly lacked.

She asked the priest which items of baggage contained his personal belongings and, after he had indicated a small and worn leather suitcase, she said a few words to the young man next to her in some sort of West Bird's Head dialect, and the latter fetched it up.

"Come with me. We will see Fr. Massimo and take you to your huts."

"I need to put everything here in order," the pilot said. "These monkeys will make off with anything that is not tied down."

"If you care to first see where you will be staying, I can assure you that these people will not touch your vehicle or belongings."

"No, no. You go on ahead. I trust these natives less than I do my own wife!"

The sister shrugged her shoulders and frowned and proceeded to lead Dom Ramiro towards the village.

The air was fresh and clean. Butterflies floated by them. The paths were muddy from recent rains and led past a kind of large communal garden that was enclosed by a bamboo fence. The place was lush with vegetables and a few people were working the ground—dicing it with hoes, poking it with shovels.

"Before we came, the people here were only growing sweet potatoes and squash. Now we have introduced tomatoes, lettuce, cucumbers, corn and cauliflower."

15

An old man, who was kneeling amidst the plants, stood up and looked over. He waved his hand and smiled and the nun waved back.

"They appear to be well-nourished enough," Dom Ramiro said.

"They eat game and vegetables. Nine months ago we brought in this buffalo which provides the village with much-needed milk."

A water buffalo stood at the edge of the village chewing lazily on grass. It raised its head and licked its lips as they passed.

The huts were made of woven bamboo, their roofs thatched with sword grass. People stood at their door-steps and watched Dom Ramiro as he went by. The men were muscular, with calm, serious eyes. Their teeth were black from chewing betel nut—a substance the population was so addicted to that their tribal name was adopted from the plant. There were almost no signs of modernity. A few people wore t-shirts or rubber sandals, but for the most part they were dressed in native garments—the men naked except for a penis sheath, the women bare-chested with grass skirts wrapped around their waists; and Dom Ramiro averted his gaze from them as if his modesty were offended.

A few chickens pecked at the earth. A little girl stood, sucking her finger. A fertility statue was tied to a bamboo pole.

In front of one hut stood a man of great age, a strange cap made of some kind of plant fibre on his head. In one hand he held a single arrow. His chest was lean and wrinkled and his eyes had a concerned, wondering look to them.

"This is the village headman, Kiafuri," Sister Justina said, leading Dom Ramiro up to him.

"He is old."

"Older than the earth," the woman laughed.

Dom Ramiro bowed towards the gentleman and Sister Justina said a few words in the language of the place.

In a slow and solemn voice the man replied, and stretching out a hand touched the face of the priest. The latter pulled back and waved the other's hand away with his.

A look of dismay appeared on Sister Justina's face.

"What is it that he says?"

"Nothing."

"As surely you have observed," stated the Portuguese, "I am a man of the cloth. The world holds few surprises for me. Give me the translation, if you please."

"He says that . . ."

"Yes?"

"He says that you are food for the forest."

"Meaning?"

"I have no idea! He is very old and day dreams a great deal. But come, let us go."

Soon they came to what might be termed the village square—a medium-sized plaza of dirt surrounded by huts, in the centre a firepit with logs placed around it to serve as benches. To one side was a structure much larger than the rest, which had been painted white and was raised somewhat off the ground with four steps leading up to a small deck. Over the door of the building the words *Deus providebit* were written on a board in blue lettering.

A tall man stood in front of the building, clutching a rosary in one hand. He appeared to be in his early thirties, had dark hair, olive features and was dressed in a cassock, his handsome yet grave face offset by his white collar. He stepped forward as they approached, stuffing the rosary in his pocket.

"Dom Duarte Ramiro I presume?"

"Of course. And you are Fr. Massimo Tetrazzini?"

"I am."

"We tried to radio you to inform you of the approximate hour of our arrival, but could not make contact."

"The radio received water damage due to a storm last week and is broken."

"An inhospitable place to be cut off from the world—you have indeed chosen an obscure location for your work."

"It is as it was created."

The Portuguese smiled grimly.

"But it is the devil who has made these people dull and no other," he said. "Their industriousness is not especially striking, and I can say the same for their outward assiduousness towards the Christian faith. Sister Justina and yourself are the only beings I have seen who have the appearance of believers—the only two I dare say who are not quite stripped naked. Can they not wear crosses about their necks?"

"Do not mistake poverty and simplicity for dullness," Fr. Massimo replied. "Undoubtedly the people here would not fare well in Rome or Paris, where treachery is considered an asset and greed a virtue. But it is here that they live. I have little doubt that modernity will soon enough encroach on these forests and force what you call industriousness onto these people, but for now let them be quiet. Adam also was naked until Satan made him feel shame. One should not judge a people's goodness by how they are attired or bedeck themselves. Christ himself carried no cross about his neck and neither did John the Baptist. Vali will show you to your hut. Please refresh yourself and rest up. I will have a chicken plucked for our supper."

Dom Ramiro gave a sour grin by way of reply and let the young man lead him to a hut, which was apparently newly built. The floor was of rattan. The place was small and simple, but clean. A narrow bed with a mosquito net about it sat in a corner. There was a crudely fashioned table above which a cross made of bamboo was placed.

Vali set down the priest's bag.

"You are good here," he said in English, and left.

Dom Ramiro looked around with an expression of dismay. He then fell down before the cross and prayed for the salvation of the souls he had seen that day and for God to give him the strength to do His work and for the conversion of heretics and schismatics.

2

THAT evening, Dom Ramiro, Fr. Massimo, Sister Justina and Manuel sat down to eat in the refectory, a medium-sized hut to the right of the church, furnished with a single long table of teak, and in one corner a smaller table on which sat a short-wave radio, the section of roof above it showing evidence of recent repair.

The dining table was laid with a chicken, manioc root, a tomato salad, and, to drink, sweet sop wine. Outside, in the village square, the villagers were sitting around a fire, smoking pipes, chatting, telling stories, laughing.

"The Patntrm are not shy," Dom Romiro observed.

"They are enjoying themselves," the pilot said; "we might as well also."

He poured himself a cup of the wine and, after taking a drink, began eating rapidly; eyes wide, jaws active.

The Portuguese took a bite of a chicken wing that was on his plate and tampered with a slice of tomato, but did not seem disposed to try the other fare which, though not as humble as what some desert fathers might have eaten, seemed less appetizing to him than locusts or horse fodder. His eyes rested on a small lizard that was clinging to the wall, before he began:

"As you realise, I was sent by the Pontifical Mission Guild, with direct authority from Rome, and letters of authorisation from the Archbishop of Jakarta."

"Yes."

"In Europe and America the number of believers has been consistently on the decline. Young people, seduced by the wiggling thighs of exoticism, turn to Buddhism, Sri Baba, or sometimes throw themselves into the profanities of Rudolph Steiner or U.G. Krishnamurti in the false belief that it will bring them closer to God. Armed with sophism and scepticism, they are more difficult to convert than dead trees or demons. The Lord's work now lies in the outbacks of Africa, along the Amazon river and here, in the wilds of New Guinea."

"There is room for charity everywhere," Fr. Massimo said.

Dom Ramiro, ignoring the other's words, proceeded:

"This land must be tamed, its people introduced to the luminous rays of the Holy Spirit and its rotting jungles transformed into a heavenly country. The name of our Redeemer should be on the lips of all. I understand there is a village not far from here where there is some sort of pernicious activity at work. It is under the command of a false preacher."

"Roy Tombuku," Fr. Massimo suggested.

"Yes, that is him."

"He is in the Awi village, around forty kilometres east of here."

"They are not Christians."

"I do not know what they are. I have been near the village, but have not entered it. I am of course aware of Roy Tombuku, but have made no effort to see him."

"So your reports indicated. But you are here to bring the locals under the command of the Church. Wheat does not grind itself into flour, and men are not proselytized without the Good News. You must show them the friendship of Christ."

"That is the only reason you think might have brought me to this place, proselytization?"

"Well, you are not here for the wine," Dom Ramiro ejaculated nodding his chin towards the beverage they were drinking.

"Indeed I am not."

"Then you might offer some explanation. We are, after all, doing battle against God's enemies. You have been here for over two years, yet the residents of this place give little indication of progress. And it would appear that you have made no effort to bring the surrounding villages under His dominion. The previous resident of this place, Don Renzo Bazzoffi, disappeared, and you seem to have done little to honour his memory. I understand that being out here at the edge of the world you must feel a certain liberty, and it is easy to grow lax, but you must not forget that you are ultimately answerable to Rome."

"Fr. Massimo does most excellent work," Sister Justina ventured.

"How many baptisms have been administered? How many have you confirmed? How many come to mass to receive the Eucharist and how many do you confess?"

The questions were met with silence.

"There is more to good work than just baptisms," Sister Justina presently began. "Fr. Massimo has administered to the sick, helped them develop the garden you saw, and in all his activities put their human happiness and dignity foremost. I have been teaching a few of the children to read and write in English and——"

Just then a village man burst into the room, interrupting the nun. Falling to his knees, he talked very rapidly. His face wore an expression of great concern. He made a desperate gesture with his hands. Fr. Massimo and he exchanged a few tense words.

"What seems to be the problem?" Ramiro asked.

Fr. Massimo replied. "This man's wife, Binel, has fallen ill. Something happened to her while he was sitting around the fire. I must go and attend to her. Please, stay here. I will be back as soon as I am able."

"No," said the Portuguese, "I am not here to sit idle. I will go with you and see what it is all about."

"As will I," Sister Justina added.

"Not me," said the pilot, filling up his cup with wine, "this chicken might fly away if we leave it uncared for."

The rest of the group got up from the table and followed the man through the village to the hut in question. A number of Patntrms had gathered outside, and were conversing in low, troubled voices. The priests and nun entered. The place was lit by a small wood fire which burned in the centre of the room. A woman was there, lying naked on the floor, apparently in the heights of some sort of paroxysm. She twisted this way and that, agitated her groins, her arms moving like snakes and legs kicking and trembling. A thick grey foam was bubbling out of her mouth, the lips of which were distorted, rigid. A hissing sound came from her nose. Next to her stood an old woman who was saying something in a falsetto voice. Sister Justina went to the victim and grabbed her hands, which she found to be extremely hot.

"It is like Siti and Papei," she said.

"What is this?" Dom Ramiro asked Fr. Massimo.

"It is the third case of its kind in as many weeks," the Italian replied. "It is a variety of sickness that afflicts these women, the origins of which I have as yet been unable to trace. At first I thought it was dysentery or some sort of encephalitis or rabies, but no longer believe this to be the case, though it may well be of a zoonotic nature."

"What happened to the other two?"

"Unfortunately, they perished."

"It is the work of the opposer. There must be many evil forces in this land, which is surely nearer to the Pit than any other."

Fr. Massimo did not reply, but moved towards the young woman, knelt and shone a flashlight in her eyes. They were glazed over, the pupils excessively dilated. He murmured some words of concerned sympathy and she, jolted to her feet as if under the influence of some electric current, leapt towards the fire, grabbed up a burning stick, and thrust it deep into her mouth.

There was a strange, crashing noise, but no one could determine where it came from.

Binel spat out the stick and let out a whining scream. She threw herself on the ground in agony, swinging her legs in the air. Fr. Massimo, assisted by the woman's husband, grabbed her and held her down.

Dom Ramiro shook his head in disgust and left the place. Making his way back to his cabin, he passed by the firepit. The men were no longer laughing, but sat chanting some song in low, sombre voices—undoubtedly some variety of incantation for the sick woman.

Later in the night, he was awoken by the sound of the village dogs howling.

3

THE next day was rainy—water running from the sky from morning until late in the afternoon. The woman, Binel, had died during the night, and the village was in mourning for her. Her husband shed tears and beat the muddy earth with his fists. He cut off his beard and tucked it under her left armpit and then they dug a hole in the mud about a quarter mile from the village and buried her.

Father Massimo said a few words in Patntrm dialect, a rough translation of the canticle *Benedictus*, and Dom Ramiro planted a cross Sister Justina and he had constructed at the head of the grave.

Fr. Massimo, Sister Justina, Dom Ramiro and Manuel then returned to the refectory. Over lunch, the Portuguese brought up the subject of visiting the Awi village.

"We will go there tomorrow," he said.

"You wish to fly?" the pilot asked.

"How many men can your helicopter hold?" Fr. Massimo asked.

"No more than three, myself included."

"Then we must walk. Going with only three men would be unadvisable. To arrive by helicopter anyhow might well be too much of a spectacle."

Dom Ramiro agreed to this and Fr. Massimo called Vali in and, after explaining the expedition, asked him to gather together half a dozen men and make preparations for the next day.

"To the Awi, to see Roy Tombuku?" Vali said. "He is a bad man. There are many bad men there. They will be unhappy when they see us."

"And I doubt very much the sight of them will bring us much joy," Fr. Massimo replied. "But we will go all the same." And then turning to the Portuguese: "The important thing is to bring gifts. Nothing will be accomplished without them."

"No need to worry there," Dom Ramiro said. "I have gifts enough brought just for this purpose."

Later, when Fr. Massimo returned to his room, he sat down at his desk, rolled a cigarette and lit it. Before him were numerous notebooks he had filled over the last few years—odes he had written on the implications of knowledge, observations, reflections, a list of words found in the New Testament but not in Homer, descriptions of plants, customs and people. And so it is that isolation is the nourishment of intellectual brilliance, and those interludes fortify the spirit so that it might be prepared for exertion.

"It seems that my period of contemplation has been broken," he thought, wishing truly that he who had been in the highest position did not have to obey such a low, narrow-minded fellow as Dom Ramiro.

4

THE next morning a party consisting of Fr. Massimo, Dom Ramiro, Vali and six strong young Patntrms set out for the Awi village. A few of the latter carried spears, the others machetes. Two were given heavy packs by Dom Ramiro, which he said contained items meant for the Awi. Fr. Massimo handed Vali a rifle which the young man slung over his shoulder.

"You trust him with that?" Dom Ramiro asked.

"He is one of the few in the village who knows how to use it. He has made himself something of an expert shot. I would sooner trust Vali with my life than almost any man I know."

They walked for about thirty minutes in silence, and then Dom Ramiro spoke:

"It is most unusual that you have a woman here as your assistant. A nun no less."

"Sister Justina is the ideal associate. She has a great heart. She gives love to the people of the village and is loved. The situation was arranged by the Bishop of Padua."

"And though I am not one to contravene orders coming from so exalted a sphere, I do find it troublesome. For temptation comes also to the godly and without some higher authority to directly watch over your actions . . ."

"Every man has a higher authority—within himself. In the Vatican itself, egregious sins are often committed, while a lone hermit, without affiliation to any creed, can sometimes be in direct communication with the Eternal One."

"If you are going to start talking about the goings on in the Vatican," Dom Ramiro said in a peevish voice, "I am afraid we will begin to argue rather quickly. I am no stranger to the place, having been summoned there twice, and have the greatest respect, not only for he who sits on the throne, but also for all those cardinals around him, whose good intentions should no more be questioned than those of the archangels—of Raphael or Gabriel who support the sacred ladder by which we climb up-high."

"The people here are in need of more than just good intentions, be they of angels or men, who are both subject to immersion. Loggers encroach on their forests and miners dig into their mountains. The benefits of modernity—education, medicine and ease of life—are denied them, while its disadvantages are heaped on them in great portions. Streams and rivers are polluted with acidic runoff from the mines. Trees are cut down and people displaced. Stay among us here for a short while at least before passing final judgement."

They climbed over rocks and down into little valleys—indeed, it seemed they were either climbing up or climbing down, and the terrain was anything but hospitable. Dom Ramiro was surprisingly nimble and scampered along with great agility, determined not to fall in the rear of the group. The Papuans who had to carry the packs struggled somewhat under their loads, and Fr. Massimo was curious what they contained.

At one point the Patntrms stopped at a buah merah tree and each picked one of the bright red fruits which they, however, did not eat but carried with them, to the surprise of the Portuguese.

Eventually, they started making a steady ascent and gradually rose out of the forest and onto a high ridge. They stopped and looked around. The scene was beautiful. Begonias were in flower. A large river snaked through the jungle below. Clouds slowly made their way across the sky in front of them, looking like bizarre lizards or dragons. In the distance were seen mist-covered peaks. Nearer, the tops of the huts of their own village could be seen and the clearing where the helicopter rested—a strange and incongruous object stranded in that sea of nature.

Crossing over the mountain, however, the scene immediately changed. Mute obscuration, a hematophagous sponge. The sun no longer seemed to shine and a heavy, morose feeling hung over the land. Strands of yellowish mist floated through the air, which itself seemed chilly and inhospitable.

"An unpleasant environment," Dom Ramiro commented.

"The side of the mountain we came from the Patntrm people call Good Mountain. This side they call Bad Mountain."

It was easy enough to see where the names came from. One side of the mountain had a cheerful feeling, the other seemed hostile, depressing—some dark and hungry atmosphere depicted in hard, somewhat brutal colouring. The greens seemed dull and blurry. The recesses of the valleys looked black and forbidding.

Below, in the distance, about ten kilometres away, they could see a few thin trails of smoke rising out of the forest.

"That is the Awi village," Fr. Massimo remarked.

The Patntrms, who until then had been exchanging words every now and again in a jolly enough manner, fell silent. Vali took the rifle off his shoulder and held it in apparent readiness and the group made its way forward, over a way that was somewhat more rocky, steeper.

Descending, they came upon a cave of sorts, the entrance of which was surrounded by carved wooden images, of humans and animals—giant fish and men with one eye—fetishes made of grass and branches—rocks with faces painted on them—logs with mouths gouged out and smeared with red.

As the Patntrms passed, they deposited the buah merah fruit they had picked before the place, each saluting the dark cavern with a short bow before passing on.

"Is this place a primitive temple?" Dom Ramiro asked.

"The people of this area believe that it is an entrance to the underworld," Fr. Massimo explained, "and that the spirits of the dead enter here. It is an offering of sorts they make, so that if they or any loved one should die, they will have something to eat on their trip to the next world."

"The naïveté of the aboriginals is an unending source of amazement. A handful of ugly fruit will do their souls little good in purgatory; and the place of judgement must certainly be far away from this savage land."

"Or access to the underworld might be had from here as well as Mount Etna—for the Architect of All Things surely was aware of the concept of a back door—and it has also been said that there are many entrances to the underworld, some being small holes under rocks, others dark and wide caverns in mountains, or again some being situated in the midst of swamps."

To this the Portuguese did not answer, but merely shook his head and smiled indulgently.

After traversing the steep incline, they were plunged into a forest which became so dense that they could only proceed with great difficulty. The Patntrms chopped away at vines and tangled shrubs and the party pressed onward. Out of the earth, enormous trees rose up which seemed like giant pillars that held up the very sky. The leaves at their feet moved and a huge centipede was seen arching along the ground. A branch whispered and a serpent was apparent as it sank its fangs into some incautious bird.

Passing through a clearing, they saw a rock on which rested what appeared to be a number of human skulls. The Patntrms silently exchanged glances and walked on with grave faces.

"Some sort of tomb?" Dom Ramiro asked.

"No. The men believe it is cannibalism."

"The Awi?"

"It is hard to say. The Awi have violent tendencies, but that does not mean that they are man eaters. And yet it is distinctly possible. But there are also many other tribes, some of them nomadic, who are surely in the habit of eating men."

Dom Ramiro made a pained expression with his face and moved on.

After they had proceeded for another hour or so, Dom Ramiro noticed that there were figures walking far to the left and right of them—stepping silently through the dense vegetation—a flicker of bicep, a distant sidelong glance.

"We seem to have attracted notice," he remarked.

"They have been following us for the last fifteen minutes," Fr. Massimo replied. "Our presence was probably detected some time ago. These are the Awi. It is their way of letting us know that we have crossed into their territory and are not trusted to do as we like."

As they proceeded, the men came in closer, so Dom Ramiro could clearly observe them. They were tall fellows, and carried crudely carved wooden rifles the bayonet-like tips of which were sharpened and painted red. These they brandished in an aggressive manner. They wore strands of sedge in their hair and had raised scars on their chests and shoulders in the shape of stars and aeroplanes. Around their necks hung necklaces of canine teeth.

The situation was somewhat tense. The Patntrms proceeded silently, looking straight ahead, as if the escort was not there. Vali held his rifle close to his body and had a determined look on his face. And in this manner they proceeded for around half an hour until they came to the village, which consisted of five or six large clan houses, having the appearance of the hulls of upside-down boats. Each one probably held forty or fifty individuals. There were a large number of dogs about the place, which were clearly being bred for food, as one was right then being butchered by two women in grass skirts, who gazed at the intruders malevolently as they passed. No one else was in the open, and it seemed that they were held up in the long houses as, looking over, Fr. Massimo could see movement behind the thin walls and imagined that hundreds of eyes must have been staring at them.

The impressions received were certainly neither friendly nor hospitable. No gardens or signs of joy. Only the dogs, which came growling and nipping at the intruders' feet, and an abundance of flies which came and buzzed about them and settled where they could—a turmoil of jaws and shrill wings.

In the centre of the village there was a large wooden cross, painted red, which Dom Ramiro looked at with surprise and curiosity before being hustled along with gruff words by the Awi warriors who exuded an aggression that was anything but reassuring.

"They are taking us to Roy Tombuku," Fr. Massimo explained.

"Good," the Portuguese coughed out. "I want nothing better than to see this charlatan who encamps this questionable crucifix here but reveres not those who are the messengers of Iesus Nazarenus for whom our hearts thump and bleed."

Before the largest of the clan houses, which was towards the end of the village, was a platform raised about a metre off the ground. On this a man was sitting cross-legged.

He was lean and muscular and wore a white mask, with openings for the mouth and eyes, an old peaked colonel's cap on his head that looked like a remnant of the Second World War, and a sort of sash across his chest that gave him a military bearing. In his right hand he held a lit tobacco pipe, from which he would pull every now and again. In his right hand he carried a knife, the hilt of which had three electric plugs hanging off as tassels. On his left breast was a large scar in the shape of the Mons Star.

It was Roy Tombuku.

Fr. Massimo's predecessor, Don Renzo Bazzoffi, had been the first to send reports concerning the Awi headman back to Rome. He had, so he said, met the man, and indicated that his influence was pernicious—that the fellow was an agent of evil, whose pedigree tended strongly toward the demoniac. Whether he had seriously attempted to convert either Mr. Tombuku or any Awi was not known, as, around the time Don Renzo Bazzoffi's reports became most pressing, the good priest disappeared.

Fr. Massimo had been sent as his replacement, but by and large he had confined his activities to Patntrm Village, and let most other prospects in the neighbourhood well enough alone, as he had not come to that remote location in search of ferment or to thrust his religion onto others, but rather as a place of contemplation where he might forget the intrigues of Rome and practice the religion of Christ.

Roy Tombuku spoke rapidly, in a deep and aggressive voice that Dom Ramiro could not help but feel somewhat frightened at. Fr. Massimo conversed with him for a few moments before reporting to Dom Ramiro.

"His language is not far different from Patntrm. He asks why we are here. He wants to know why we are invading his domain."

"Tell him we are here to bring him God and offer him and his people the benefits of a spiritual birth, to demonstrate to him the joys that can be gained from faith and repentance. We offer them the opportunity to abandon sin and mend their ways and find that salvation which is offered free of cost by our Lord and Saviour Jesus Christ."

Continuing to act as a translator, Fr. Massimo relayed the message.

"Your god Jesus Christ?" An ugly type of laughter came from behind the mask. "He is good for you white men. But our ancestor is his brother Gakobus Wenge, who is stronger, has eighty stomachs and forty heads. When he comes with his cargo of rifles and goods, the world will be ours again and men like you will only be fit for pulling lice from the backs of our dogs."

"The cross in the centre of your village is a symbol of the Lord Jesus Christ, who was born and died for our sins," Dom Ramiro said, holding up his rosary, so its crucifix was apparent. "He was nailed to this cross and then placed in a sepulchre where, after three days, he rose from the dead. I am His messenger and bring you good tidings!"

The headman stood up in anger. The pipe fell from his hand.

"What? Your god?!? That wood belongs to Gakobus' lady, Queen Biktore. Our protectress. She lets us sit on her breasts in the space between life and death and can eat our enemies with her vagina, which is so hot it can cook taro. Have you come to steal our gods? Have you come to kill our gods? Do you think you can overpower my raifols? Your heads are worth little here. You came uninvited, but you will leave invited, and if you return, I will personally chop you each into six parts and enslave your souls."

Roy Tombuku waved his knife about and the electrical cords shook.

"A rebellious fellow, isn't he?" the Portuguese said.

"I believe now would be a good time to bring forward your gifts," Fr. Massimo suggested in an even voice.

"Um, yes."

At a signal from Fr. Massimo, the Patntrms set down their loads and began to unpack them—but to the astonishment of all, they contained nothing but books—cheaply printed bibles in the Tok Pisin language.

"Bibles for people who can't read," Fr. Massimo murmured, examining one.

"It will give them the incentive to learn." Dom Ramiro said brightly and, taking up five or six, set them down at the headman's feet. The latter looked at them curiously for a moment, picked one up and leafed through it. A sound came from him that seemed like laughter, but he then threw the book down in anger and began to yell—eyes wide behind the mask, a revelation of spatial depth—throwing his arms about in a flurry of frantic geometry.

"He believes that you are making fun of his ignorance," Fr. Massimo said.

The headman pointed to one of the Patntrms, a fellow by the name of Saá.

"Raifols, take that one!"

Two of the militiamen grabbed and held him as he moved his shoulders from side to side and struggled.

"Release him!" Fr. Massimo cried.

But his request was ignored. One of the militiamen began to stab the unfortunate fellow with his "rifle"—in the sides, belly and chest—blood oozing out and staining Saá's body primary magenta, some ferocious springtime—the poor fellow letting out a gasp, a request for assistance.

Vali lifted his gun and fired a shot at the assailant. The bullet entered his left cheek and passed out through the rear of his head and he fell back, dead. The militiamen, momentarily alarmed, released Saá, who collapsed to the ground. Two other Patntrms went up and grabbed him. From the doorways of the nearby houses a few people began to appear, staring at the scene with grim curiosity.

"Come," Vali said, "let us be gone from here before we are all dead."

With great haste they began to exit the village.

Roy Tombuku leaped from his perch and, pointing after the party, cried out in a stern voice, indicating that the retreating individuals were enemies of Queen Biktore and had come to cut off their cargo—to block it with their books of spells.

The militiamen began to cautiously pursue and men and women to pour forth from the long houses in great number. Some held spears, others bows and arrows. The women who had been butchering the dog let off their work and, with bloody hands which held knives, joined the others. Slowly they advanced on the party.

People spoke, one to the next, beginning to agitate themselves into a fury with harsh, serrated voiced. The dogs of the village began yelping. Several of the men began to kick at the earth. A woman screamed. Whipped laughter and the entrails of tension. The whole scene was chaotic.

Dom Ramiro moved one leg before the other. Vali covered their rear with his rifle.

As they fled, arrows were discharged at them. A second Patntrm, one of those helping to carry Saá, was shot through, and so both men were left behind—dead or dying at the edge of that unpleasant village, since to attempt to carry them out would have been extremely difficult—almost suicidal.

"Do you think they will follow us?" Dom Ramiro asked in a frightened voice.

"Unless we give them a reason not to," said Vali.

"Then, unfortunately, that is what we will have to do," was Fr. Massimo's sorrowful remark.

The young Patntrm took careful aim and let off his gun. One of the militiamen fell, a bullet having pierced him just below his left eye. Fr. Massimo had been right. Vali was an exceptionally good shot.

The crowd of Awi stood back momentarily, anger in their faces as they stared at the body collapsed before them.

"Another," Fr. Massimo suggested.

"Yes, Father."

Another bullet was fired, this one landing on the chest of one of the largest of the militiamen, whose eyes opened in astonishment as he saw blood shiver out of him. The Awi retreated, pushing and tripping over each other. Roy Tombuku was yelling furiously, pushing himself before his justifiably frightened people, shaking his strange knife in rage.

The party of priests and Patntrm hastily made their way away from the village. Vali snapped off a few more shots as they went, not to hit anyone, but to let them remember that he was armed. It did not seem, however, that they were being chased. The real rifle had proven more horrible than the wooden.

After about three kilometres they slowed their pace and water began to leak from the sky; some tears bestowed by heaven on the failures of men.

They trudged on solemnly, without words, water rolling down their backs, their feet occasionally slipping in mud. The day had turned out to be a bad one and the Patntrms looked at Dom Ramiro with hostility, deep sadness, and definite distrust. Fr. Massimo moved forward in silence, a frown carved on his face.

When they finally reached the village they were wet and tired and in low spirits. The relatives of the slain were informed of their deaths, and there was a great commotion. Hands were thrown in the air, wails let out, a woman fainted. Kiafuri came out of his hut, pointed to Dom Ramiro and Fr. Massimo and uttered some words of reprove.

"We are a people of peace. Why have you broken our harmony? You and your unhappy god brought us this trouble."

Fr. Massimo frowned and, staring at the ground, murmured, "There is none good, but one."

The Portuguese went back to his hut, stripped off his wet cassock and, with a bed sheet wrapped around his body, prayed long before the cross, while Fr. Massimo did what little he could to comfort the families of the dead—but it was little indeed, since he could not bring them back to life, and he felt at least partially responsible for having taken them on that useless mission—one that he had known from the beginning to be a mistake. That the families did not even have the bodies of their loved ones was a point as well. A few of the men spoke of returning to retrieve them, but Fr. Massimo convinced them that such would be folly and only result in more deaths.

"This will bring trouble," Vali told him. "The Awi will, one day or another, come and look for our heads."

"They are warlike, and feast on unhappiness."

Vali smiled grimly. "We could be more warlike than them. If we had twelve or fourteen more rifles, the forest would belong to us."

"The forest already does belong to you. It is your head that I am concerned with."

5

THE next day at breakfast Dom Ramiro spoke.
    "We will be going deeper in, to the north," he
said. "Though I hardly find the work amusing, I have
been asked to plant the cross where it is not."

"Do you not feel that you have done enough *good*
for the present?" Fr. Massimo commented.

"Yesterday's incident was unfortunate. But I hardly
feel blameworthy for it. That I was somewhat naïve, I
will admit. But you had not adequately apprised me
of the situation. How was I to know it was a tribe of
devils and not men? Should I be scared away from my
sacred duty? If Peter had not gone to Rome, we would
still be kissing the toes of Jupiter and pretending that
the future might be read through the greasy entrails of
certain birds."

"The area to the north of here is one of the most
remote in the world. None of the villagers here have
ventured there. Though close at hand, to the Patntrms
it is as remote as America or China. It could be unsafe," Fr. Massimo ventured.

"I have little doubt that it is so. But we must get to these creatures before the Muslims or the Protestants do if the true Christ is ever to have a foothold out here."

"What exactly is your intent?"

"It is said there are tribes that are completely secluded."

"This I believe to be true. The nature of the landscape in that direction is such that travel from one point to another can be difficult, to say the least. Cliffs hem in valleys and thick jungles seclude mountains. To travel by foot through the area would be madness."

"I would like to make an aerial survey of the place. We need to see who is in need of civilisation, of Christianity—of the Gifts of the Spirit."

"And initiating contact?"

"We will see."

"Because," Fr. Massimo said, "there are uncontacted tribes, to be sure. But if they are uncontacted, it is likely because they wish it that way."

"Showing people what is good for them is never an easy task. It has, after all, taken us two thousand years to get this far. For the present, however, we will simply fly over, looking for a serene population in need of salvation. After that, we will see."

Three days later, when Dom Ramiro had been adequately rested from his previous adventure, he, Fr. Massimo and the pilot climbed into the helicopter, a group of Patntrms watching with great interest.

The weather was clear, the sky a brilliant blue.

The engine was started and the propellers began to rotate rapidly. The Patntrms waved as the machine rose up into the air and began to move in a north-easterly direction, like some great and agile bird swooping out of sight—over a crest of hills that acted as a frontier to the unknown.

Fr. Massimo gazed out at the lush vegetation below, at the surging expanse painted over in green. The terrain, viewed from that height, was something awful. Steep mountains rose out of the jungle. Rivers plummeted into the depths of dark forests, dug through, forming deep gorges, wound around odd-shaped hills and threw off diverging tentacles which waved about before breaking into mazes of small streams that disappeared under dense canopies of trees. It was an awe-inspiring sight—the Earth as creation had made it, a tapestry of fecundation oozing with arabesques of cosmological herbs.

"Better to fly than to be walking through that," Manuel commented.

Dom Ramiro interpreted the forest in his own way: "One day, in the not too distant future I would hope, we will bring civilisation to this place, replacing this unmanageable tangle with industry. Paved roads will pacify this violent chaos and well-built towns with well-built churches will give the population the opportunity to contemplate God before his Only Son returns to reclaim the Earth. Yes, the jungle is a place of slithering serpents, of unspeakable sin, and must be eradicated—made clean and manageable, a place where even virgins and children are safe and lambs may roam about without fearing the hungry jaws of wolves."

The voice of the Portuguese was hardly audible above the engine, and neither the pilot nor Fr. Massimo requested him to repeat what he had said.

They all three observed the terrain, trying to catch sight of some habitation, but they saw none. The helicopter swooped over a deep valley and then, after gliding upwards toward a mountain top, turned and headed west.

"There is nothing here but trees," Manuel said to Fr. Massimo.

The latter shrugged his shoulders. The view was beautiful and the intricacy of life below exhilarated him. He had no idea if they would see people, but hoped, if there were some tribes, that they would not. Let them be undisturbed. There was little that Dom Ramiro or his Tok Pisin bibles could do for them and Fr. Massimo had little faith in the former's ability as a messenger of Christ.

The chopper swung over the tree-tops; zig-zagged back and forth over the forest. The three men fell silent, gazing at the monotonous drama beneath them—each glad that they were high above instead of submerged in those emerald waves.

Manuel thought of home, where he hoped to be returning within the next few days or week, well paid for his time away—and he would eat and drink much, kiss his wife, pound the mattress with a few prostitutes, and then sleep for a fortnight.

The Italian thought of times past and what future might come—considered if it truly was God's work he was doing or that of Azazel. For doing nothing seemed often to be much more in accord with peace than doing that which could, in all possibility, cause pain to others and even to oneself—and he had, in his time, known much about this.

Presently, he did catch sight of a clearing in the distance and movement. He thought he saw human limbs and was about to say something, but instead pressed his lips tightly together. He looked at the pilot, whose eyes were buried behind sunglasses, then glanced at Dom Ramiro, whose gaze was fixed in a different direction.

The Portuguese turned his head to the right. His eyes opened wide. He began motioning frantically with his hand.

"There are beings down there!" he shouted above the noise of the engine, thrusting his finger downward. His face wore an awful smile. The cubes of his yellowish teeth seemed to almost dance in his mouth.

And, indeed, a number of men, whose bodies seemed to be daubed with some sort of white paint, giving them a fantastic appearance, stood in the clearing, waving spears in the air.

"Fly lower," Dom Ramiro commanded.

"It might be better not to," Fr. Massimo suggested.

"No, I want to see these naked heathens."

The pilot did as instructed, circling back around and descending within about thirty feet of the group which was made up of twelve or fourteen athletic-looking men. One of them began gesticulating violently. Another thrust his weapon towards the machine. The whole group was shouting. The helicopter drew nearer and a spear, with great precision, was hurled at it, ricocheting off the windshield. A second flew before their eyes, while another came very near to entering the cabin. Most in the group carried a number of these projectiles, and they began launching them in rapid succession—fearlessly thrusting out their chests in challenge. A few others had bows and arrows, and taking careful aim, shot them at that giant bird that roared above.

The pilot, seeing that the situation was a dangerous one, steered the machine upward and away and soon the indigenes were out of sight.

"There are your future Christians," he joked as they soared away over the treetops.

"A close escape," Dom Ramiro said in a tense voice.

Manuel was silent for some moments as he gazed at his instrument panel.

"Or maybe not," he said presently, pointing to the fuel gauge. "Look at the needle—our fuel line must have been hit."

"Can we make it back to the village?"

"Impossible. We're losing gas too quickly. We'll have to land."

Manuel veered the machine off to the left, down into a valley of sorts, and managed to set it down in a very constricted meadow. He got out and checked the engine.

Sure enough, the fuel line had been hit and gasoline was spilling out onto the ground. He quickly repaired the leak with some silicone tape he had in the helicopter's tool kit, but by that time the tank had been for the most part drained.

"Do we have enough fuel to return to Patntrm Village?"

"No. We probably only have about twenty litres, which wouldn't get us far. And if we run out during flight, we risk crashing into the tree tops. This machine isn't going anywhere."

Manuel turned on the radio and tried to get a signal, but after thirty minutes gave up.

"We are too far away from any point of contact," he said. "And being grounded certainly doesn't help. We would be lucky to get a signal in the air, but down here—impossible!"

"There is little for us to do then," Fr. Massimo said. "Our choices are either to go and look for help or wait for help to come to us."

"But it might be something other than help that comes to us," Dom Ramiro suggested.

"Any idea of the distance back to our village?" Fr. Massimo asked Manuel.

"Maybe a hundred and fifty or two hundred kilometres. Through this jungle though, it's like a thousand. We had better stay near the chopper and wait for someone to come for us." He grinned sadly. "If anyone comes for us that is."

"Sister Justina knows the direction we went in," Dom Ramiro said. "When we don't return . . ."

"When we don't return, there will be nothing she can do," Fr. Massimo said. "The radio in the village does not function. The only thing she can do is wait until the Archdiocese of Jakarta sends someone along. But this is Indonesia. Help will not be quick to come. And she only knows the general direction we went in, which consists of thousands of square kilometres of forest. Finding us would not be easy."

Dom Ramiro clenched his fists.

"Well, for the moment we seem to have no other choice but to make the best of—of the situation. Lord have mercy upon us. Doing his work is not always a simple thing."

"The day is already far advanced," said Fr. Massimo. "So, for the present at least, we stay. When given a chance to demonstrate one's virtue, one should be pleased."

This decided, they set about making themselves as comfortable as possible.

Fortunately there were a small amount of supplies in the helicopter. Fr. Massimo took some rocks and prepared a firepit. The pilot went to the forest's edge and gathered some not quite dry wood. Soon the sun was setting. As it grew dark, they built a small and rather smoky fire and ate crackers, sardines and Garuda brand coated peanuts. There were two blankets. The pilot took one and Dom Ramiro the other—acting as selfish men do—the instinct for survival, for keeping one's own skin warm, overpowering any compassion for their little community as a whole. Manuel drank from a bottle of arak that he had and held his pistol on his lap.

He laughed. "We might die out here."

"Christ will protect us," Dom Ramiro said as he pulled his blanket tightly around himself.

"He has not been doing a very good job so far."

"No one can understand His plans."

"A drink?" the pilot offered the bottle to the Portuguese.

"Just a sip to keep out the cold."

Fr. Massimo laid down and closed his eyes—listened to the two men exchange comments—and around them the sounds of the jungle and the sounds of the night—the chirping of insects—something moving through leaves in the distance—the piping sound of some unknown creature—frail clicks buoyed by an unfolding domain of bruised reverberations. A night that brought out more life than the day—a life that gloried in sluggish shadows and the marrow of darkness.

"I hope I can get my chopper out of here," Manuel was saying. "Getting grounded like this was not part of the bargain. I'll have to be reimbursed. My time. And my wife. Me being gone so long . . . unnecessary risks . . ."

His voice droned on for a period, as he sipped from the bottle, but presently, probably drunk, he fell asleep.

Dom Ramiro looked at the surrounding forest—at trees reaching out their arms and the dark shape of bushes hunched about. He recalled the men he had seen, who had hurled their spears and shot their arrows, and wondered where they were—if they were stalking through the jungle now, looking for them.

He had an unpleasant sensation of fear. He thought of the Saviour who had died on the cross and hoped that Papua would not be his cross, and that he would survive—be able to return to Portugal to live out his days in civilisation and comfort. Yes, maybe the apostatizing lifestyle was not for him. He gathered up the bottle of arak in his hands, screwed off the cap, and lifted it high—drank until his throat and stomach were burning and soon after closed his eyes, let his consciousness tumble through the forest of the night—pursued it would seem by some carnivorous impulse, some primeval compulsion which the sawing sounds of crickets and the thrusting prick of stars drew forth—a nostalgic urge of immobile dreams that, peeled back, revealed the gleam of crimson flowers.

His life dripped around him, pushed against him, and he could almost smell it, like a dish of curdled milk—what a hard childhood! He had been weak. His father would take him to the Matadouros Oliviera de Azeméis, and when they killed a cow ask them to fill up a cup with hot blood for the boy to drink. And he remembered that warm liquid, how good it tasted as it ran down his throat and filled his belly with comfort, the laughter of the men at the abattoir as he wiped the blood from his lips and begged for more—some homicidal river down which he was floating, emerald-coloured crocodiles gliding by him, their jaws open, jagged wombs of quiet, dripping lust and overhead some black, sweating sky he could touch, push against with his hands and he was frisking along over a landscape of oily bones, looking for something with great desideration.

6

WHEN DOM RAMIRO opened his eyes the next morning, he saw himself in a forest of naked legs. Sitting up, he realised that around a dozen men had formed a circle around them. The pilot and Fr. Massimo were already awake, the former holding his pistol in readiness, the latter seated calmly stirring the coals of the fire. Another three or four Papuans were by the helicopter, tapping it with their spears and feeling its smooth surface with great curiosity.

The men, who were tall and of sinewy build, for the most part carried long bamboo bows. They had strips of red-dyed pig skin inserted in their ear lobes and were otherwise naked except for a groin shell. By means of wild honey, beeswax and animal fat, their hair had been formed into braids.

"Don't be startled," Fr. Massimo said. "If they had wanted to kill us, we would already be dead."

Dom Ramiro shivered. The morning air was cold and the bad dream continued.

"They are the ones we saw yesterday?"

"No."

"What shall we do?"

"See if they can help us."

Fr. Massimo rose to his feet and held up his hand in a gesture of peace.

One of the men spoke, raising his bow in the direction of the sky and then pointing towards the forest.

Their language seemed to be a type of Waioli or Kao, and though very different from that of the Patntrm, Massimo was able to have rudimentary conversation—understanding about every third word of their speech and making himself understood in turn.

"He says they are of the Maki tribe, the Long-Ears, and that they will take us to their village."

"Is it an offer or a demand?" Dom Ramiro asked.

"Would it make any difference?"

"I won't go with them" Manuel said, fingering his pistol. "If we leave the helicopter, we will never be rescued."

"If you fire that pistol," Fr. Massimo replied, "you will get us all killed. Put it away and be calm. Even if we stay by the helicopter, it could be weeks before anyone finds us—if they ever do. By that time we will have run out of crackers, I can assure you."

The pilot hesitatingly did as was suggested and he too rose to his feet. He gave one last sorrowful look at the helicopter, took up the unfinished bottle of arak, and then turned his back on it.

They walked through the forest, the Papuans proceeding with apparent caution. Whenever any of the three tried to speak, they were signalled to be quiet; so they stalked forward like hunters looking for game.

After the party had proceeded for about seven kilometres they came to a river which they forded, water coming up to their knees in algid wetness. Once on the other side, the Long-Ears grew somewhat more relaxed and spoke a few hushed words amongst themselves and to the white men and with patience Fr. Massimo was able to understand the situation.

"They are worried about the Up-River People," he explained to Dom Ramiro.

"Up-River People?"

"Some sort of hostile tribe. It seems a number of their warriors have been spotted in the area. These fellows are scouts who were out looking for the invaders."

"They seem quite formidable. It surprises me that they would be afraid of anything."

"Yes, whoever this other tribe is, they must be of an especially violent nature. They might have been the people we saw from the air. It is, I believe, fortunate for us that these Maki found us, as we will likely be safer with them than camped in the bush."

And, after proceeding for another three or four kilometres, they did come to the Maki village—a friendly looking place exposed to the copper-coloured sun, flanked on one side by a large taro garden with a few mounds on which were cultivated bananas.

The group was greeted by the inhabitants—old men coming and gazing on them with wondering eyes—mothers holding babies to their breasts and smiling. The women wore some kind of bright yellow powder in their hair that made it like gold, and lent them a striking appearance. People approached them with pleasant looks on their faces, gazing at their apparel, leaning over cautiously and touching their boots, clearly impressed by the toughness of the leather.

Any trepidation that the three visitors had, soon disappeared; they felt their lives secure and their stomachs grumbled for refreshment.

The houses were spear-shaped constructions built on stilts. A number of plant totems were placed about the place. In a very small shelter in the centre of the village was a mummy. It sat on a low table of sorts and was totally black. Before it were placed a few orchids, apparently as way of offering.

Dom Ramiro gave Fr. Massimo an enquiring look.

"That is their ancestor, a type of god they worship," the Italian replied. "It has probably been sitting there for generations. It is like the incorrupt saints we keep on display in our churches."

"Though this fellow hardly seems incorrupt, and is indeed less handsome," Dom Ramiro added with typical cynicism.

They were taken to the hut of the headman, whose name was Hokowe. He was a large, plump fellow, who sat surrounded by around twenty women, of varying ages and degrees of beauty.

"They are his wives," Fr. Massimo said in an undertone to Dom Ramiro.

"These people lead a life of fornication and violence it would seem, thrusting their spears about during the day and at night rolling in a sea of flesh."

"I hardly think we are in a position to be criticising his lifestyle," the Italian suggested. "We should be grateful for their help."

One of the warriors explained to Hokowe how they had come across these three strangers seated in the jungle, next to a large yellow monster that would not move.

"Who are you?" the headman asked.

Fr. Massimo bowed slightly and proceeded to attempt to converse, making clear their situation as best he could.

"You saw the Up-Rivers?" Hokowe asked.

"I believe so."

"How many?"

"Maybe fourteen."

The headman appeared thoughtful. He nodded and, with some words spoken in a mellow tone, and a wave of his hand, indicated that the three strangers were welcome. The youngest of his wives, a somewhat frail individual whose name was Lé, then served them good water. While they drank, Hokowe turned to the Portuguese and said something which the latter did not understand, but, taking advantage of the situation, produced his rosary with its dangling cross and showed it to the headman, who frowned, shook his head and murmured a few words.

"What does he say?" Dom Ramiro asked.

"He says that it is bad luck and that you should bury it."

"Nonsense."

"One man's heaven is another man's hell."

The three foreigners were provided with a guest hut and given fruit to eat and that evening Hokowe hosted them. A pig was brought out and an arrow shot through its heart. Its tail was cut off, dipped in its blood and then planted in the taro garden. The pig was roasted and served with sago balls, Fr. Massimo being asked to carve the meat. Though the food was by no means good (the pig was undercooked), all three ate with relish, as they were quite hungry, and it was warm and nourishing.

There were two large firepits. One around which the women and children sat, the other, the men. Hunched around the fire, food in hand, the warriors relaxed. Smiles eased their stern features as they chewed on meat and chatted—telling anecdotes, jokes, commenting on the bizarre costume and physique of their visitors, who to them seemed like some strange clowns or humorous spirits whose fragile limbs needed to be protected from the elements and whose speech was like sharp sticks.

"None of them seem to have ever seen white men before," Dom Ramiro said.

"It appears not," was Fr. Massimo's reply. "To them we must look rather pitiable."

"We are," the pilot said. He stuffed a piece of pork in his mouth. "Today they are serving pig, but tomorrow it might be one of us."

"Do not exaggerate," said Dom Ramiro in an uncertain voice.

Fr. Massimo held his peace, wondering himself how they might extricate themselves from that village and somehow find their way home. He determined that the next day he would broach the subject with Hokowe and see if they might secure a guide to lead them in the proper direction, at least a day or two's trek. He was hopeful that, before too long, he would be back in Patntrm Village, tending to the garden, speaking with Sister Justina, enjoying the small comforts of familiar surroundings.

A young man sitting near Fr. Massimo, who introduced himself as Huga, asked the former:

"What is your trick?"

"My trick?"

"You must have one."

The priest smiled with a certain degree of sadness, thinking of tricks and the trouble they had caused him.

Manuel was covetous of his arak, sipping it alone while the villagers indulged in some rude and intoxicating drink of their own. Broad strokes of laughter in a sulphur lake. The lukewarm perfume of a pearl grey waxing crescent. The pig was reduced to a pile of bones, its skull looking like a torn rag, its vertebrae like rare gems. A few drums were beaten on. A man does five or six dance steps.

Hokowe rose to his feet. He walked about in a circle, lifting his knees high. Then he stopped, flung his arms in the air and, with a sound like crickets coming from his mouth, emitted a greenish beam of light from his back.

There were murmurs of approval from the bucolic spectators.

"Witchcraft," Dom Ramiro said.

"An impressive though rather useless feat," said Fr. Massimo.

Hokowe strutted about, flashing the light here and there; and then, with a snap of his fingers, let it expire.

As the evening drew on, he tried to press women upon them, but Dom Ramiro, with agitated gestures of his hands, let it be understood that they in no way could accept such hospitality.

Hokowe laughed and suggested that the two priests must be married.

"No," Fr. Massimo said, pointing to the sky, "we are men of God. Our hearts belong to Him."

The eyes of the Long-Ears opened wide. Two or three grinned in a sceptical manner.

When the pilot finally understood what was being offered, he thumped on his chest and pointed to a woman.

"Me, me, I'm a man!" he said with an ugly gesture.

The Long-Ears were amused. The headman had one of his men fetch a short dumpy looking woman who smiled tenderly at Manuel. The latter shrugged his shoulders and rose from his seat.

"Leave this woman alone," Dom Ramiro said. "You are a married man and are not here to have pleasure with the local trulls."

"You were paying me for flying you around. Thanks to you I lost my helicopter. You can keep your morals and I'll have my fun. When it comes, I take it."

60

And so the two were sent off to lodge under a net of palm fronds, the Long-Ears shouting congratulations after them, clearly amused by this absurd union.

Fr. Massimo and Dom Ramiro then retired to their own hut where, after praying to God, they soon fell asleep.

7

A huge rat scampers along the forest floor. A parrot scratches itself. A stroke of yellow sunlight bleeds over the horizon and is transformed into an exquisite pink by emerald leaves reflected in the eyes of chaste stones.

In the early hours of the morning there was a sudden eruption of sound—violent shrieks, strange howls, the patter of men running past the guest hut in confusion—an alarm which threw the two priests out of sleep and onto their feet in a moment. Rapid, fearful conversation could be heard without—a prism of buzzing broken by a shrill cry.

"Some sort of assault seems to be underway," Fr. Massimo said in a quiet, sharp voice.

"The Up-River People?"

"It must be."

And, indeed, it was. At dawn, when the village was still in deepest sleep, the invaders had crept in, terminating a few men who had been on guard, thrusting their weapons into the naked flesh of the sleeping Long-Ears, giving them no opportunity to prepare themselves and attacking with a savageness that was like some hurried current that swept happiness away. The Up-River force—warriors whose bodies were painted with white stripes along the arms and torso so they looked like skeletons; faces painted to appear as skulls—was made up of only about fifteen men, who carried spears, bamboo knives, a few bows and arrows, two or three stone-headed axes, but they had the advantage of surprise and an unmitigated blood lust that filled the Long-Ears with panic. Most ran or sat trembling in fear, and the few who tried to defend themselves were quickly cut down.

Of this latter, Fr. Massimo recognised one of the Maki who had led them away from the helicopter—a muscular young man who now pierced one of the Up-Rivers through with his spear. Another of the invaders stepped up and the two struggled for several moments before the brave young man fell dead, a drastic knife wound flashing from his throat.

A woman cried out as she was punctured by an arrow. A spear was hurled through the neck of one man. The head of another was split open by a stone-headed axe.

Manuel came out of his hovel wearing nothing but underwear and carrying his pistol.

"Bastards!" he yelled.

He shot one of the invaders two times in the chest, then turned and fired a bullet right between the eyes of another who swung back, life swept away. He was preparing to shoot a third when a smallish Up-River crept up behind him and buried a spear in his back and he fell a dead man, his face set with an angry, horrified grin, blood throbbing out over his side.

A few Up-Rivers approached the priests, at first with the intention of killing them. But when they saw their white faces and black cassocks and recognised their docile manners they seemed to reconsider and instead prodded them with their spears into the centre of the village where, guarded by a tall fellow with an axe, they stood as onlookers.

"Let us run," Dom Ramiro suggested.

"It would be better to pray," said Fr. Massimo, and falling to his knees proceeded to do so, calmly, as a man willing to accept his fate. Dom Ramiro grasped his rosary and, taking his fellow-priest's example, with trembling lips recited Ave Marias—murmuring those words that the angel Gabriel had used in praise of the Blessed Virgin Mary, mother of God, mother of Jesus Christ.

Fr. Massimo wondered, if death should now come to him, whether he should use his transference of consciousness abilities or not—but did not dwell on this too long, as his heart was full of sorrow at what he saw; and presently the Maki headman, Hokowe, was herded up next to them, his nose bleeding, his eyes expressing affliction. Due to his weight, he had not been able to run fast enough and had been apprehended.

"The world is over," he said. "This world now is over."

And Fr. Massimo, looking on at the carnage, could not help but think it was true.

That red-handed parade of dissilience; a battle both quick and bloody. Though the Long-Ears were by no means weak, they were by nature peaceful, while the Up-Rivers took a joy in killing that seemed almost lustful—flailing about in an orgy of crushed raspberries and smiting timid flowers. The aggressors only lost about six men while at least seventy villagers were killed outright and another thirty taken captive and herded to the centre of the village where the two priests and headman were. The rest managed to escape into the jungle, where they were undoubtedly hiding in fear.

The invaders strode around the place, glorying in the carnage they had caused, their eyes feasting on the gore with delight.

They spoke a completely different language than anything Fr. Massimo had heard and expressed themselves generally in curt monosyllables which could only be understood through inference. One of them, however, an individual shorter and less muscular then the rest, knew a few words of the Long-Ear language, that he had picked up who knows where.

He approached one of the wounded Maki and spoke to him.

"Name?" he asked, kneeling down next to the man.

"Toku," the other replied, a look of the most profound fear on his face.

The questioner turned back to his comrades, repeating the other's name in a jeering manner.

Then, turning again to the wounded man.

"Be quiet. We friends," he said in a gentle tone. "Friends. Friends."

The other seemed somewhat reassured and smiled weakly.

At this, the Up-River lifted his axe and, bringing it down with a vicious swing, quickly began to hack the other's head off, and then, grabbing the severed object by the hair, raised it, dripping with blood, triumphantly for all to see. A few of the Up-River people let out horrible chuckles. But to most the scene seemed hardly worthy of notice as they were each involved in cutting off bits of flesh from the dead that lay about and chewing them, raw, in a hideous display of conquest.

Dom Ramiro turned away in disgust. Fr. Massimo lowered his head and said a silent prayer for the slain Maki—for this human who had died without apparent reason, due to some pivot of evil that the Italian could not say he fully understood.

After the group of Up-Rivers had gorged themselves, their jaws dripping with blood, they made preparations for departure. Each one hacked a limb off of one of the dead. They then rounded up the living—those who had neither escaped nor been killed. Most of these were women, or the weaker-looking men. Any male that looked too well built, they killed outright.

Presently they began discussing what to do with the two priests. They were clearly impressed by their appearance and judging by their gestures and expressions, might well have considered them to be some sort of delicacy—or something magical—or something to be dealt with with consideration—that pair of human bats whose faces were cold vapour.

Toward midday, they urged them and those Maki who they had not slaughtered into the forest, to make the voyage back to their own village. Loathing was clearly boiling in Hokowe. He moved when he was prodded, but his motions were full of pride. He gazed at the Up-Rivers with a disdain that they seemed utterly immune to.

The march was long and hard. The Up-Rivers walked at a very rapid pace, forcing their captives on in the roughest manner—jabbing them with spears in their thighs if they lingered—cursing them and striking them with their fists when they stalled.

They primarily went along the banks of the same river the priests had crossed the day before. At one point they came to a high waterfall and had to climb up the side of a cliff. A few times they were forced to enter the forest, which was dense and dark, with strange spiders hovering on leaves and the occasional serpent festooned over a branch.

The Long-Ears wept as they walked, apart from Hokowe, who maintained a grim silence.

The Up-Rivers now and again would slice a piece of flesh off the limbs they carried and chew it as they went and Dom Ramiro blinked and saw it all through dewy eyes. He could not help but imagine them eating his own muscle and fat, and he held his arms close to his body as if to protect them—imagining their teeth ripping into his sinews, grating against his humerus.

"What will they do with us?" Fr. Massimo asked Hokowe.

"Nothing good," was the reply.

"They are going to kill us," the Portuguese whined.

"They might," Fr. Massimo said, "but they have not yet. So you have something to be grateful for."

Dom Ramiro tried to reply, but the only thing that came out of his mouth was a sort of groan. If they had not killed them yet, the reason seemed obvious enough: they could only eat so much at a time and it would be easier for them to take them home and slaughter them there, as their appetites decreed.

He walked on, trembling, nauseous, drowning in the thick mucous of fear and regret.

After about six hours hard trek, they began to ascend into the true highlands—the vegetation became less dense—they walked through gorgeous open meadows of knee-high grass—through conifers and rhododendron heaths. The air was brisk. Fr. Massimo looked about him almost with pleasure, and wished he were able to enjoy it at his ease. The horror of the march was in sharp contrast to the surrounding beauty, and the priest could not help but think, as he looked over the grandeur of the landscape, that their predicament seemed unreal.

But then his thigh was touched with the point of a spear and the stinging pain made him conscious of how very real it all was.

Towards evening, when the sun was just beginning to set, still following the river's course, they found themselves treading through a dark and dolorific forest made up of *Papuacedrus* and ferns, and then finally arrived at the village of the Up-River people—a dirty, unpleasant place—situated in a clearing near the base of a cliff-face—an area seldom struck by sunlight, pushed up against on one side by the cool, damp rock-face, on the other by the backside of the forest, and it would seem that the founders of this little town had gone out of their way to find the most cheerless place in the area. No gardens could be seen. The dwellings consisted of nothing more than lengths of upright bamboo, supporting vertical lengths of the same with palm leaves draped over the top—constructions which only served as the most rudimentary protection from the elements. They were arranged in clusters, without apparent thought and a disagreeable odour hung about the location—an odour of decay, of defecation, that made the captives squint and twist their faces in apprehension. A large number of human heads, in various states of decomposition, were stacked into a pyramid of sorts in what might have been termed the centre of the village—a medium-sized patch of dirt with a few firepits in it—and others hung from bamboo poles placed about at random—and there were other poles, of a great height, the purpose of which was unclear. Bones, of humans and other animals, were scattered here and there. There were a few upright totems and then one immense one, carved from a giant log, that lay, one end resting on a large stone. This latter log had a slit running down its side, and Fr. Massimo recognised it to be a slit gong drum of enormous proportion. The only hut that was different from the rest was that of the headman, which was of better construction and decorated with the skulls of crocodiles—an ominous looking dwelling, the only of substance in the place, its outer walls fortified with shields of bark on which designs, of staring eyeballs and faceless mouths, were scrawled in ashes.

Fires were burning and the smell of smoke was in the air. The captives were able to see the Up-Rivers without their paint, in a domestic context.

This tribe, undoubtedly due to the seclusion in which they lived—a seclusion quite understandable when the consequences of intercourse with them were considered—were strikingly different from other Papuans that Fr. Massimo had seen. They had slender noses and somewhat pinched features—their gazes were haughty and disdainful—their faces seemingly wrinkled beyond their years, yet endowed with an intensity that could best be described as violent. The women were naked except for a net they wore over their heads, a type of veil made from tree bark fibre which entirely hid their features. The faces of the men were morose, their eyes hostile and somewhat pink, like beings who had always been far away from joy—who lived sequestered in a realm of butchery and battue—of repellent conquests and sinister glory.

The arrival of the returning group and their captives produced a great excitement in the village. The women giggled and, nudging each other, pointed at the victims, while the children danced around waving bones.

70

The headman of the place, whose name was Saragigi, came out of his hut and approached the group with a slow stride. He was a ferocious looking individual, with a long, thin head. He wore grass armlets and through his ears were thrust hog's teeth, while his nostrils were pierced with the talons of a falcon. In one hand he carried an old, dried-up human head, and in the other a wand of bird-of-paradise feathers. His features were stern, his eyes of an almost bluish colour, his gaze penetrating and meditative.

He inspected the prisoners. First he scrutinized Hokowe with an evil look; then examined the two priests—looking at their pale skin with great interest. Pointing at Dom Ramiro, he said something and everyone laughed.

"It seems they like you," Fr. Massimo murmured.

"O splendid days," the Portuguese replied with quivering sarcasm. "It has always been my heart's desire to be popular amongst cannibals."

"The alternative is to be unpopular."

After being studied in the manner of prize cows at a fair, the captives were led into a group of filthy little bamboo cages, blood dripping from the unprotected thighs of the Long-Ears due to the prodding they had received during the trek.

The cages were situated against the cliff face, their doors secured by wooden pin locks of surprising sophistication, the key of which was held by a tall and muscular individual with a frowning, cruel face.

Hokowe and the two priests were caged together, separated from the other captives, who were in turn

71

divided into several groups, the men put apart from the women. Dom Ramiro broke down and began to weep, crying out that he should have never come to that awful land and that God had clearly consigned it to hell and would never show mercy to those who gathered on it. Fr. Massimo did not attempt to comfort him. It had, after all, been the intention of the Portuguese to tamper with these people, to bring them under the wing of the Church, and if the results were contrary to expectations, he had no one to blame but himself.

Hokowe sat gloomily silent, as one immobile in shame, accepting some hypnotic fate that left him useless.

The Italian thought of trying to comfort him, but what could he say?—and so set his back against the bamboo ribs of the prison and scrutinized his own mind—wondered how peace could be found in such a place, in such conditions—wondering if this cell, with its evil aromas and confined space, could teach him something. He recalled the words of Father Moses, the Robber of Nitria, who had said that to gain wisdom one must be like a three-day-old corpse.

"Only by abandoning all hope can I hope," Fr. Massimo said to himself.

And in that place, it seemed easy enough to be without hope.

8

THE next day the village was full of dingy excitement.

The cage that Fr. Massimo was in was situated in such a manner that its inhabitants could make out clearly the activities of the village.

The women made several large fires. The children wrestled with each other in a remarkably violent manner. The people spoke little, but it was apparent that they were making a great preparation. Some gathered in wood, while others dragged out gruesome looking totems made of bones, mud and dried grass. Large earthenware pots were placed on the fires and the women began to cook some sort of preparation. A few men climbed up the poles and, balanced at their heights took out ropes made of grass with rocks tied to the end and began to swing them rapidly in space— an activity which they kept up with great endurance for hours on end.

Towards mid-day a group of men began beating on drums and chanting a lugubrious melody—a lurching music that was constantly grabbing out and pulling back—a group of ferocious birds pecking and gurgling—a naked march over treacherous thorns. Its enharmonic quality had something profound to it, stirring as it did certain primordial chords wet with the dampness of time, and filling the two priests, particularly Dom Ramiro, with trepidation.

"It seems to be some kind of celebration," Fr. Massimo said.

"But what do they have to celebrate?"

"Perhaps their victory over the Long-Ears."

The Italian asked Hokowe about their fate.

"Your fate I cannot pretend to know. But today I will travel from the Earth to the Sky. This world is gone for me." And, for the first time since their horrible adventure began, he smiled—a smile at once sad and ebullient, like an acrobat performing in a graveyard. "I will spend some time amongst the night stars, and enjoy the hospitality of their embrace, and I will be fed by those who came before me—a meal of sago of boundless sweetness."

Late in the afternoon, the Up-Rivers took Hokowe and four male Long-Ears of the strongest appearance out of their cages, but left the two priests and the remaining Long-Ears. The former were led to the celebration and placed in a row before the totems.

The men on the top of the poles now undid the rocks from the ropes, let the latter drop to the ground, and fastened the ropes to the top of the poles. Then, taking hold of the loose end of the ropes, they began to swing about, first letting the ropes wind around the pole, then unwind, the whole soon being done with dizzying rapidity, the men letting out high-pitched cries as they soared above the village.

Saragigi came out and the people stopped their chattering and the men at the top of the poles stopped their swinging and slid to the earth. The headman wore a giant crown of bark that was painted with elaborate patterns—his face and body were covered with white paint. In one hand he carried his wand of bird-of-paradise feathers, in the other an axe. By his side were two others. One had his fingers shoved in rods of sharpened bamboo, so his hands were like great claws. The other was a tall and muscular individual whose face was obscured behind a mask made of bound-together grass, and in one hand he carried a large, stone dagger.

Fr. Massimo recognised in this person the keeper of the key, and indeed saw that implement secured to the waist band of this latter's grass skirt.

"Owarbwa," Saragigi said, addressing the first man, "do what you must."

The first man approached one of the Maki, and without prelude, plunged his clawed hands into his chest and plucked out his heart, which he proceeded to eat with the utmost relish—gnawing at a shapeless mystery, glittering cramoisie drizzling down his tufted chest.

"Arok," Saragigi said, addressing the second man, "do what you will."

The tall man then approached another. After thrusting the dagger into his throat, an act which killed him almost instantly, he began to butcher the fellow with great skill, taking the first cuttings and placing them as offering before the totems and then tossing the subsequently carved flesh to the audience who scrambled for it as if it were prizes spilling from a piñata, a cloud of dripping tongues refreshing themselves on those lonely clods.

Hokowe cried out and advanced on this strange priest, on this man known as Arok, but a few Up-Rivers rushed out and held him back. The other two warriors who had stood with Hokowe came to his assistance, but they were struck down, murdered in a scene of confusion.

It was then that Saragigi stepped forward.

The Long-Ear headman stood upright, his gaze tranquil, ready to meet his fate. Saragigi yelled at him—then laughed—then yelled again and with his mouth still open wide began to suck, his breath somehow drawing Hokowe in; and like a long draught of smoke, he entered Saragigi's mouth. The latter stood triumphant, cheeks expanded, while a voice came from within—the voice of Hokowe—and his cheeks seemed to be pushed at, here and there, as if someone were trying to grapple their way out.

Saragigi exhaled a colourful plume, which instantly took the shape of a stunned Hokowe.

The Up-River headman then gazed over his people who were silent before him, said something to them and then, raising the axe, he let it fall on the other's head. Hokowe collapsed to the ground, his cranium split in two.

The people gave a whoop of approval and then one of Saragigi's wives approached the corpse and began rummaging through the brain. With a sign of victory, she plucked out some small object, and held it above her head proudly—a kind of nut—a stone of sorts that glistened red in the sun, a slaughterous gem that cried a few tears of blood down her arm.

This small pit was brought to the headman with great ceremony, all falling silent during the process. He tossed it in his mouth and swallowed, like a man eating a candy and, seating himself on the ground, proceeded to gorge himself with Hokowe's flesh, his body swaying from side to side as he apparently descended into a sort of ecstasy—and it was with this that the celebration proper went into effect.

The bodies of the victims were first singed over the fire and then, after carving them up, the flesh was wrapped in banana leaves and put over the coals to cook. These the people grabbed up and unwrapped, eating the contents with a pleasure that overpassed the sensual.

Scraps of meat were thrown to the children and they took them and hurried off with them, greedily rushing into the shadows.

The hands seemed to be most prized, and were given to the highest ranking men, who ate them with great pride, gnawing at the meat, sucking on the fingers, and casting the bones aside, to move on to other choice parts, while the women and elderly were excluded from the best and the very weakest merely chewed at the parts cast off by the rest of the group;

a nervous ritual of hierarchy under the sway of terrestrial magnetism, the strong pushing to the clouds, fragility dragged to the dirt.

At a certain point Saragigi began to reel about, performing a short, quaking sort of dance. He took a stick and tossed it to an onlooker, who in turn broke the stick in two. The headman then took it up and placed the two ends together and lifted it up—to all appearances whole again. He then snatched Arok's stone dagger from him and ran it through his own hand, but it simply slipped through, without causing damage. He waved the hand above some bones and they began to dance about. Then a ray of green light swung out from his back—the very light that Hokowe had possessed—and all present let out a roar of delight.

Dom Ramiro watched all this with a kind of fascination, before finally hiding his face in his hands and murmuring broken prayers, in Latin, Portuguese, appeals to God, Jesus, Mary, and all saints, expecting at any moment to be pulled from the cage and eaten, for the place where Hokowe had sat just a short time before was now empty, his physical body now food for cannibals; and the noisome feast rolled on in a descending order of appetite; the Up-River people got pleasure from devouring their prey; gorged themselves on human flesh and became drunk on that beer the women had been brewing in their earthenware pots, from old fruit, *Boletus manicus* mushrooms and kava—an evil liquid the vile smell of which the prisoners were aware of from where they sat. Their eyes grew wide and they stumbled about in some kind of ecstatic dance—lifting their legs, thrusting their arms in the air, wiggling their fingers and baring their teeth—as if they wished to climb up to the sky, catfish who had grown hind legs or ferns who had developed thumbs—the intoxication seeming to have linked them to all creation, from the immense pressures of the earliest phases of the universe, to its ultimate expansion, when gods and demons were scattered to the heavens and hells. A sky of shattered bones and a wheel of moon and the celebrations continued deep into the night. Finally, exhausted, they sat and lay about in an atrocious euphoria, as beings locked to nature with invisible chains.

9

SEEKERS of truth, mobility slain, a limbless dog that forgets how to howl; and so life for the two Europeans was anything but pleasant. Flies and mosquitoes buzzed about them. They were constantly harassed by the villagers—stared at—teased by the children and spit on by the men. When it rained, they were wet. Their toilette was nothing more than a declivity at one end of the cage, and they were forced to dwell amidst their own stench, like some species of autocoprophagic ants.

The Up-River people did not only eat human flesh. They also ate roasted bats, lizards and mice—in truth any sort of meat they could get hold of, though they seemed completely ignorant of or averse to vegetables; the carnivorous diet undoubtedly effecting their mental state, where their lives could only be continued through the cessation of others.

The horse is stronger than the wolf; the elephant grander than the tiger; and indeed it is that a diet of strict meat makes one bellicose, predatory, full of hatred and cut off from compassion—conniving and dishonest, mean and supremely selfish—for what could be more selfish than extinguishing the lives of other creatures in order to extend one's own? And there is certainly a point at which meat consumption is no longer a matter of simply nourishment, but a matter of conquest, of grand egotism.

Dom Ramiro was miserable, frightened, seemed half crazy—nervous with a dire expectation—the expectation of one condemned to die, but denied the ritual of date, the consolation of civil authority.

"They are going to eat us," he kept murmuring to himself. A few tears slithered down his cheeks.

Fr. Massimo on the other hand was completely calm. Even in the confined space he managed to do exercise—push-ups and sit-ups—stretches and static holds—doing his best to keep his muscles strong and body limber.

"I have time," he thought, "why should I waste it."

Hair spilled from his chin; his fingernails stretched themselves out.

He engaged in contemplation; sat cross-legged, his eyes staring straight before him. Supported by equipoise in a lopsided situation—the weight of awfulness pulling, straining against his sure suspicion that harmony was the origin of all things, even chaos.

Death did not frighten him. He had died before. And, in any case, he still held the power of transference of consciousness, which he could use should he need to and conditions permit—that power he had, in his previous form, learned from that manuscript by Simeon ben Jochai, *The Just Treatise of Transposition*.

And, being gobbled up by a tribe of cannibals was not of course the way he would choose for his present body to meet its end—and if there was any chance to get himself free from that place, he would take it. Meanwhile, he would look within himself, gaze at his soul—search out its beginning—try to comprehend who it belonged to, what it was made up of—whether it was a whole that could not be divided, or something made up of parts—and in these meditations he saw his soul or self flowing like water—saw it as some ethereal substance that seemed to come from the distant past and be headed to the far beyond, leaving a type of moisture along the way. He saw it jumping about, anxious, splitting apart and then dancing toward some odd vertex—an eye cloaked in diaphanous purple—an object that could neither see nor be seen, which retreated when looked at and advanced when ignored.

Through the bamboo he kept track of Arok, the one who had the key, and wondered how he could get this from him; wished he might find a way to free himself and the other captives.

An Up-River woman came often and through her veil stared at them, particularly Dom Ramiro, for long periods. Her face was covered with the net, but by the appearance of her body, her well-shaped limbs, she must have been attractive. She would come early in the morning when most of the village was still asleep, squat before their cage for as long as an hour, her field of vision centred on the Portuguese, and then depart—all without so much as a syllable coming from her lips.

"She seems to be partial to you," Fr. Massimo observed.

"So much the worse. I feel as if she were looking at a roast."

And the Portuguese, shutting his eyes, would mentally recite his disconnected prayers—Hail Marys and the Holy Rosary—a Devotion of St. Joseph and a Te Deum—Marian prayers and prayers for help against spiritual enemies—one receding into the next in a desperate monotony that left the priest's mind transfixed yet unsettled, like a Diptera clutched by a single wing. He tried to fall back on his belief, but the gravity of fear sucked him along, plunging him away from the mighty hand of God, from tenderness to blind electricity, a thrusting delight in blood yet unthought, a hand grasping at oily red aether.

Dom Ramiro had been born in Carregosa, Portugal, the only son of a dealer in devotional statues—a small man with rather frightened eyes and a soft, nervous voice. The boy's mother had died when he was just a baby and he had been brought up by his father and the housekeeper—a woman by the name of Mafalda who was infected with religious mania and who told the boy, as he lay in bed at night, stories of saints martyring themselves—the heroics of being burnt alive or torn apart by lions in the arena—of how the blessed Peter of Castelnau had been thrust through with a lance by Albegensian heretics, and how St. Domingo Henares de Zafra Cubero had been beheaded while bringing the good word to Vietnam. And it was indeed the stories of men perishing in foreign lands that had fascinated him most. There was the handsome Dominic Ibañez de Erquicia who expired by the torture of the gallows and pit in Nagasaki, Japan, and Joachim Royo Pérez who, at the age of twenty-four, was sent to the missions of China where he did many years of good work before being imprisoned, flogged, subjected to the ankle-crushing torture, and then stuffed in a bag and stomped to death with his mouth plugged with paste.

The child had been thin and weak. Two large brown eyes wandered lost in his circular face. It was likely that, without the nurse, he would have died—but she was determined not to let the devil steal away his young soul—this small creature who, for all she knew, might one day be privileged to also receive the palm of martyrdom, some shower of boiling oil, be pinned to Heaven by darts while the angels blew their burning trumpets.

It had been, indeed, under her advice that his father had taken him to those nourishing walks to the abattoir to drink fresh cow's blood and a pail would also be filled with the liquid, which they would bring home to Mafalda, who would prepare it into sarrabulho, a blood soup, with which she nursed the frail child; and she served him raw horse flesh to give him strength, at the same time praying fervently to the Madonna, praying to a thorn-crowned Christ for him, saying she would see that he was consigned to His power if He would let him grow and gain strength.

And so he did. And the blood he had drunk daily until he was twelve—some child who wished to suck on his own scab, a leech in pants and sweater whose head was full of sour lullabies and grisly sacraments. Later, while at the Seminário dos Olivais, he had discovered the passages in the bible that forbid it and had prayed fervently to be forgiven, the blood in his mind becoming like a naked woman, a crimson lady who sprayed pink nourishment from her wound-like nipples.

10

DOM RAMIRO was horrified and sat quaking in a corner of the cage, making himself as small as possible. Fear had completely mastered his person. He could not sleep, and when he did, nodding off in mental exhaustion, his mind was invaded by horrible nightmares—of him being eaten alive, of Saragigi massaging his brains out of his skull, nibbling on them as baby pelicans clamoured for their share. When he awoke, his eyes would come out of their shells and dart about, seeing horror and evil in every object.

A boy of about fourteen or fifteen, who they had noticed performing services around the village, presented them with a pottery vessel filled with grilled tadpoles—and though these were by no means delicious, they were consumed with great avidity, and this youth brought similar food to all the cages and everyone was grateful to him.

He was not an Up-River, but seemed to be the last member of some former tribe that had been overcome, and was now there captive, acting as a slave. He had a limited vocabulary in a number of languages and dialects, probably picked up from attending previous prisoners, and rudimentary conversation was possible.

He informed the captives that his name was Tokek.

One day this same Tokek brought everyone a dish of grilled wood spiders.

"We are being fed a great deal," Fr. Massimo remarked.

"They want to fatten you. In some time, once your meat has become soft, at the festival of Gwanru, they will kill many of you. If not you personally," the boy said, thrusting his chin towards the other cages, "certainly many of your friends."

"Gwanru?"

"A forest spirit, a demon. Sometimes he will appear as a young lady, sometimes as an alligator, sometimes a vicious monster. Whoever sees him, he eats. He snacks on villagers who wander into the forest alone. So these Up-Rivers sometimes sacrifice victims and take the opportunity to eat their fill as well."

"As they will eat us."

"Maybe. You or others. Someone will be eaten."

"And you?" Fr. Massimo asked.

The boy laughed. "They will eventually eat me too, but I think they will eat you first."

"That does not frighten you?"

"No. I will go to the land of my ancestors."

"You are not in a cage. You could run away."

"Run to where? They would catch me before I got far. And even if I got back to my village, there would be only fallen huts there to greet me. My people are no longer there and so who would be my friend?"

Fr. Massimo asked about the procedure he had witnessed when Saragigi had killed Hokowe, about the thing that had been taken from his head.

"The power of a man lives in his skull," the boy replied. "The bright red pit. So, when they eat this out of the skull, they take the power."

"Power?"

"Most men have no power. But some have the big power. Many of the headmen have big power and one goes to another—one man steals from another and so forth—one bright red pit goes to another. Just as one can rip a necklace from some man's neck and put it on one's own."

"The bright red pit?" Fr. Massimo asked.

"Yes, as I said, only a few have it. Only those with the power."

Two days later, when the boy was bringing them their fare, Massimo questioned him again.

"Who are the most powerful men in the forest?" he asked.

The boy smiled. "That is easy, Kembrur, Idoai, and Po."

"And who are they?"

"Kembrur is headman of the Yuwan, of the Tree People. He has the trick of fast walking. Idoai is the leader of the Ubuhae Folk. He has the ability to go to the underworld—to come and go as he pleases. He is very powerful and it is said that he has eaten more than one hundred and twenty men. Po is chief of the Water-Bird People. He has the language trick.

With it, he can speak the tongues of all the tribes in the universe."

"Where are they?"

"Where?"

"These men."

"To the south. Everyone is to the south."

11

MANKIND lives shuttled between hope and fear, from birth hoping for the mother's breast and then fearing that it will be taken away, and later hoping to destroy the enemy, while fearing lest the enemy be the one who destroys. So it is that most consider it better to live like a dog than to die like a lion, as they quiver on the earth and slink along the streets, skeletons grabbing at their throats in a spring afternoon that has become a terror. Even clouds fear that they might turn dry and stones hope for tenderness.

After the initial feast in which Hokowe had been killed, no other Long-Ears were slaughtered for around ten days. The Up-Rivers sufficed themselves with game, small rodents and other caught creatures. Then every three or four days two victims would be brought out and slaughtered. Not in the ceremonious manner of the first feast, but merely as domesticated animals might be slaughtered and eaten.

Then, after the third week of captivity, another festival was put under way—though this one seemed even more ritualistic in nature. Late in the afternoon the Up-River men began to paint their bodies entirely black.

Fr. Massimo saw Tokek passing by and called him over.

"What is it?"

"No moon time."

"So?"

"The offering to Gwanru."

"So?"

"So it is," the boy said, and hurried on to perform his duties.

The ritual was similar to the first feast in preparation, except that also a bier of sorts was constructed. Then darkness fell and with it the voices of the Up-Rivers. The Maki in the nearby cages were filled with fear. Some cried, some hugged each other, unsure who would be selected and then it was that two women and one man were dragged out and Saragigi, Arok and Owarbwa issued from their respective huts, their forms apparent by the dancing flames of the village fires.

Arok had a stick in each hand and began to beat them together rhythmically while Owarbwa sang and agitated his body along violently—clawing at the air, thrusting his head towards the earth. The rhythm of his voice was nervous—now pleading, now demanding—receding into whimpers and leaping up in wails of infelicity.

Then two men approached the giant slit gong drum. They each held two large sticks, sharpened to points at one end, and with the dull ends began to beat on the drum. A frantic march of sound issued out—loud, forceful, intricate—and the villagers swayed from side to side, passed their liquor from hand to hand.

The male Maki was killed by Arok, his throat slashed open, and his body dragged to the bier and placed on it. Blood from his wound was smeared over his corpse and bowls of liquor were placed around it.

Owarbwa began once more to dance and sing, performing crazily before the body. Arok banged his sticks together and made a whining sound. The slit gong drum roared. Hypnotic and frenzied became the effect. A wind seemed to come from nowhere. The flames of the fires danced about wildly. Those listening oscillated their bodies and presently a cloud of dust filled the air and there was a sound like the crowing of a cock. Everyone covered their eyes. When the dust cleared, the body was gone—a trail of blood leading off into the bushes.

This filled all present with great joy and signalled for them that now they too might feed themselves.

The two female Maki screamed and their lives were taken from them brutally and their corpses divided up for cannibalisation.

Dom Ramiro looked on with fixed gaze, some horrible fascination having taken hold of him—for he had watched living beings fall apart, the gentle hands of women become like pig knuckles, kidneys of the fallen ladies plucked out and licked at like sweet honey—and this vision that he saw of liquid jacinth that flowed amongst swirling smoke was no hallucination, but rather the clean truth of the Earth that God had created, an Earth that not only gave out grass and fruit-yielding trees, but also terror and cruelty, great slaughter and trembling cowardice.

During the feast, a man came over and, after opening their cage, tossed a few scraps of meat to the priests. Pointing, he said something in an abrupt tone.

"He wants us to eat it," Fr. Massimo said.

Dom Ramiro shook his head vigorously.

Fr. Massimo put a piece of the flesh in his mouth and chewed, thinking, "Whatever is from good is good, so is evil really there?"

The Portuguese, however, refused to touch this awful food and so the Up-River man raised his club, threatening to strike him if he did not partake of the flesh. Dom Ramiro, with trembling hands, took up a piece, thrust it between his lips and began to chew it, with the utmost disgust, and was only able to swallow due to the menace of the situation.

"What do you think?" Fr. Massimo asked him.

"It is not exactly the flesh of Christ."

A few moments later the Portuguese vomited and, in the glow of light cast by the village fires, the vomit appeared to be large spiders which hurried off in every direction.

That night the Italian heard the other priest talking in his sleep, speaking about the fires of hell—words spilling from his mouth in mumbled Portuguese, parts of which Fr. Massimo could understand, parts not—but the terror in the other's voice was apparent.

The next day Dom Ramiro appeared yellowish—his skin had the colour of a kumquat. He felt sweat wriggling out of his pores and had impulsive thoughts of strangling himself, which he suppressed by means of violent mental exertions, tossing his mind upon the cross where it bled and agonized.

A few days later human flesh was again offered to the priest. This time, however, he ate it without resistance—grudgingly chewing it down as a child might some unwanted vegetable. It recalled to him vague memories—of something far away yet familiar—some distant part of himself he had forgotten. Had not he, anyhow, in the form of a wafer, eaten the flesh of Christ? But this was not the meat of either Christ or God—and then where was God? Where was that mystical and bilabiate mouth that might bestow a cooling kiss of forgiveness on his sweating forehead and make his own quivering lips repent as they sucked flavour from pure sorrow?

But the chrysalis around him began to fall away, and he felt new and colourful wings begin to stretch themselves out like the petals of an opening rosebud, and saw himself something like St. Francis of Sales, a figure carrying his own bloody heart in his hands, or again like St. Piatus, who grasped the severed and dripping top of his own head.

12

"WHAT is the matter?"

"What?"

"What is on your mind? You keep looking around as if you are expecting something."

Dom Ramiro gave a short laugh.

"What could I be expecting?" he said.

But it was clear that was in a state of nervous anticipation; and when evening fell, and once more the flesh of man was offered to him, he took it without the slightest indecision.

Truth be told, he found it better tasting than the other fare they had been fed and each time he ate it, he did so with less reluctance—or it might better be said that his reluctance turned to eagerness, some alchemy at work changing the base to the noble—and, as has been mentioned, they were given abundant enough food of other types, so it was not a question of survival as far as nourishment went, and whether or not the Up-Rivers would kill him if he did not partake of human flesh was an uncertainty—and it seemed they would kill him eventually anyhow, so it might have been some simple cowardice, some collapse of a moral structure that was by no means well-braced.

Whatever the case, he no longer cringed when some scrap of *Homo sapiens* came his way. For as the days passed, it became a habit of the Up-Rivers to throw him bits of human flesh, and a habit of his to accept them.

"May blood be sprinkled on my soul," he murmured. "May it cleanse me from sin."

"Don't eat too much of it," Fr. Massimo suggested.

But Dom Ramiro did not bother to reply, instead turning his back on the other priest and, with deep guttural sounds grotesque, proceeding to enjoy his horrible feast—a meal of cartilaginous shadows and uncooked ears. The food brought him back to his childhood—to those days when the housekeeper would have him drink blood in order to nourish his weak body and bring him back to health. He felt that this, this anthropophagic food, was what he had been craving his whole life without knowing it—not the flesh of Jesus, but the flesh of any man—cooked or raw, it did not matter, so long as he was able to cannibalise—for when he ate, he felt his whole body become flushed, with pleasure, some seedy sort of power—an ancient ritual of self-abasement, some grand esculent incest.

Just as a vampire might siphon off the blood of its victim, so Dom Ramiro had an abstract feeling that, by eating the meat of his fellow men, he was transfusing something of their essence into himself. He went from stagnation to nervous excitement. He scratched himself frantically, tore off his clothes and rubbed his naked body in the dirt; grasped at the air, mumbled irrelative phrases and then lapsed into exhausted sleep.

The Maki in the neighbouring cages eyed him with fear, for they saw the Portuguese staring at them on and off with hungry eyes, seeming to see in each one, not a soul, but a meal, not brothers and sisters in need of salvation, but breathing baskets of flesh. And when one was taken to be slaughtered, a quivering smile invaded the lips of this man who had been sent by the Pontifical Mission Guild to bring Christianity to the uncivilized and unenlightened.

Fr. Massimo observed the other priest with disapproval, but he was powerless to stop him. Mankind was not necessarily a creature that evolved. Some became animals, some vegetables, some ghosts, and this round-faced, sharp-nosed Portuguese had seemingly become addicted to the food. The Up-Rivers would laughingly throw him half-chewed toes and bits of skin and fat and watch him devour them with glee. At night, in his sleep, he dreamed that he was back in Europe, dining off the flesh of plump women, of athletes, and even once a cardinal—and the dreams were a glory of omophagous blossoms forming tremorous networks that invaded his waking hours.

"I have eaten the clergy," he said.

"You are hallucinating."

"Doing what?"

"Hallucinating."

". . . peace through the blood of . . . of . . ." and his voice trailed off; the man seeming to have receded into a state of stupidity.

When Fr. Massimo asked him a question, he replied in a monosyllable and then shut his lips together tightly. He no longer seemed afraid so much as stupefied. His eyes had a faraway look in them, and when the Italian attempted to call him back to himself, they would narrow, become suddenly cunning.

"A man must eat. He cannot starve."

"You must remember the many who lived in the desert, in poverty of both food and accommodation. If they had all eaten each other I dare say the Christian faith would have expired long ago."

The Portuguese would nod his head in a vague manner and search about for some bone to suck, then gaze longingly at the few Maki in the neighbouring cages and these latter would cringe in horror and murmur abuses at the priest.

"You are losing sight of yourself," Fr. Massimo told him.

"My—my *self*?" Dom Ramiro's mouth hung open and his eyes had a dull look to them.

Fr. Massimo saw that if they were going to attempt an escape, they should do it as quickly as possible. They might be killed from one day to the next, and Dom Ramiro's mind was rapidly collapsing.

He looked over to the cages next to theirs. One held two Maki women, whose names were Lé and Fina, the other held the young Maki whose name was Huga. All together there were just the three that remained from the raid. The rest had been eaten.

"Yes," Fr. Massimo murmured to himself, "if we are going to make an attempt, we had better do it soon."

The next day an opportunity presented itself.

A very thin young man, maybe eighteen or nineteen years old, got it into his head to climb one of the poles—for no apparent reason than to show his own ability—and swing about.

Seeing this, a number of the men of the village called for him to come down, but the fellow simply laughed and began to swing about all the more rapidly from the rope he had tied to the pole. Then, just as he was going at the most dizzying speed, he lost his grip and flew backward, propelled some distance before coming to earth and landing on his back. His body twisted in a spasm and then he lay dead.

Arok upbraided the dead body, yelling at it and casting handfuls of dirt at it; then Saragigi came along and, after being apprised of the situation, shouted some instructions. A few men, after listening attentively, took up bows and arrows and ran off into the forest.

Several women began to prepare an abundant quantity of the liquor, which they helped themselves to as they went about their task, chanting a little song as they worked.

A bier of sorts was quickly constructed of shaven branches and over this leaves were spread and the body laid thereon. It was decorated with bones and feathers and decked in flowers—piggy-pink medinilla, scarlet rhododendrons, orchids in cerise and blonde. The body was painted completely white.

In the late afternoon the men came back to the village carrying game—a cassowary, a few narrow-striped marsupials. The dead animals were strung up around the body, cut open so their blood leaked over it; and then the young Maki woman whose name was Fina was extracted from her cage and ceremoniously killed; a large portion of her flesh was cut up and set around the thin young man, by way of offering, and his body was sprinkled with the liquor as the Up-Rivers murmured some odd, jumping sort of song and proceeded to drink heavily and eat what remained of the victim's flesh.

Fr. Massimo had expected that the same thing would happen as before, with the wind and the body gone, but this did not happen, and indeed a cloud of disappointment seemed to hover over the Up-Rivers—for there was no merriment, but simply morose eating and heavy drinking, with only a few grunts of conversation; and then the night became deep, and the villagers began to rise up and go to their huts, and the priest noticed that Arok was especially intoxicated and, hardly able to walk, stumbled and lurched to his.

The few Up-Rivers that remained soon fell asleep where they were, stretching out their bodies beneath the stars.

"This is my time," Fr. Massimo said to himself in a soft voice.

He closed his eyes and saw his body as a large vase—his consciousness boiling out of it, like steam entering a cloud of mist—swimming up and prowling out.

Deep in the night, Fr. Massimo crossed one leg over the next.

Ice, which can be both seen and held, when subjected to heat, becomes an imperceptible vapour.

His body jerked. His head lolled to one side. His mouth opened.

Some moments later, the flesh of the dead man began to quake, the feet and hands to twitch. His head gyrated around; then a slight cough, some vomit. He rose from his bier, set his feet upon the ground. For a few moments he wandered about, confused, and then, shaking his head, seemed to recall himself.

To the hut of Arok he went. It was dark within, but some strands of light came through the loose walls and lay over the place. He could see a reclining figure, could hear a rumbling snore. He crawled forward, feeling with his hands, until he was so close he could feel the heat of the other's body. A dull object could be made out near his head. It was the stone dagger that Arok always kept with him. The very thin young man grabbed the hilt, lifted it high and plunged it into the man's throat. There was a gasp, a spasm of limbs, a sudden gurgling, and then he lay dead.

The form of the thin young man, the form that was now endowed with the consciousness of Fr. Massimo, of Fr. Torturo, took the big wooden key that was at Arok's side and, leaving the hut, stalked over to the cages, stepping over the sleeping bodies of a few. He went to that the priests were in and unlocked the door.

Fr. Massimo's body sat still, chin fallen to chest, lifeless—like an empty house. The Up-River gazed at it, and then returned to his bier and lay down there, amidst the flesh and flowers and dead animals.

And presently Fr. Massimo's body began to shiver, his arms whip from side to side. He opened his eyes and held his head—like a man awaking after a night of heavy drinking. He looked around. The door was open. Dom Ramiro was curled up, asleep. He shook him and the Portuguese awoke.

"Come," Fr. Massimo whispered, "let us go."

"Go?"

"Away from here."

"But the meat is here."

"Remember, you are a priest. God will not stretch out His hand if there is nothing to grasp. This world is not yours."

Dom Ramiro chuckled softly. "You are wrong," he said—and then suddenly became voluble, words spilling from his trembling lips in ugly clods and oily beads. "I have finally found my world. This food—it is my only salvation. The host, the sacrificial victim offered by the Church, is nothing but wheat flower and salt—the sacramental beverage, nothing but the fermented juice of grapes. It is the true bleeding flesh that must be eaten, genuine blood that must be tasted, in order to perceive beyond mere metaphor." He looked off into the distance, at some world that only he could see—a world built out of stygian debris, with sun, moon and stars carved out of bone and suspended by raw tendons—skeletons hoisting themselves upon crosses made of swine's flesh and naked tongues dancing savagely as they drooled rivulets of crimson spittle.

"But if you stay, they will eat you!"

"And if they do? Then I will live on—for every drop of my blood is as a world."

The Portuguese rolled over on his side and closed his eyes and Fr. Massimo looked at him sadly, but there was nothing he could do. Dom Ramiro had apparently lost his mind and would have to be left behind.

Fr. Massimo went from the cage. It was odd to feel his legs in motion, to be able to stretch out his arms as high as he liked. To the cages near theirs he went, to those which contained the last two captive Maki. Huga's cage he unlocked. The young man stirred and looked up at him in amazement. The priest put his finger to his lips.

"Let us go," he whispered.

"Go?"

"Escape."

The process was repeated with Lé and the two followed Fr. Massimo, the three stepping quietly through the village. At the bier they stopped. The Italian gazed at the body of the thin young man he had inhabited for a short time, as a man might gaze at a suit of clothes he had been about to purchase, but which, unfortunately, were not quite the right fit.

"All earthly things are indeed temporary," he thought, and then, with the utmost caution, made his way out of the village, the two Maki tagging behind.

At first they went cautiously, quietly, but when they were some distance from the village, went as quickly as they could, running through the *Papuacedrus* forest. The river was there, and they stopped for a moment and drank from it.

"If I head due south, I should eventually be back home—or at least eventually see some landmarks I am familiar with," Fr. Massimo thought. "If I recall correctly, this river runs in a southwesterly direction, so to begin we would do best to follow its course."

The other two had not exercised their limbs as Fr. Massimo had in his cage, and for them progress was more difficult.

"My legs hurt," Lé said.

"We are slowing you," was Huga's comment.

And it was true. A strong temptation took hold of the priest to leave them behind.

"Hurry," he said. "Do your best. Our lives depend on it. We must follow the river."

There was a three-quarter moon out, but walking in the dark through the unfamiliar country was still by no means easy and their progress was much slower than he would have wished. They came to an open glade which they dashed across, then descended a series of rolling hills which progressed into forest. They kept the river to their side as best they could, though often having to scramble over hills and claw their way over rocks or through thick underbrush to do so. At a certain point, the night became darker than ever, but gradually it began to lighten. The horizon to the east began to glow, and the sun pushed itself above the hills.

It was about two hours after dawn that they caught up with them—just as they were beginning to make their way out of the high country.

Looking over his shoulder, Fr. Massimo saw a number of figures—probably a dozen or so—moving silently through the forest behind them. The Up-Rivers ran with great agility and determination. This forest was their home and they were clearly at the advantage.

"I cannot go any faster!" Lé said in a frightened tone.

"And I cannot go any slower," Fr. Massimo thought.

One pointed at them, and the group of Up-Rivers fanned out in ardent chase. A few arrows were let fly at them, which fell short. It was clear that they had no intention of capturing them alive.

The two Maki struggled, Huga panting, Lé stumbling; but Fr. Massimo offered them no assistance. He could not carry them. He could not drag them. And he dared not stand and put up a fight he could never win.

He heard a cry and turned his head for an instant. Huga had fallen, pierced by a spear, his life extinct.

The Italian raced through a riverbed filled with tremendous boulders, which were clothed in thick, slippery moss, around which cold water swam. He heard another cry of pain and knew that the other Maki, fragile Lé, had been killed.

"Now you must truly save yourself," he thought.

A spear flew by his side and, a moment later, another darted by his head. Then spears and arrows began to fly in fast succession, to his right and left, over his head and between his legs—miraculously missing his actual body which flung itself forward with as much speed as it was able.

He veered off to his right, dashed amidst the trees, tore through the bush, his heart racing.

Fortunately Fr. Massimo was in an exceptional physical state, and even his confinement had done little to diminish his strength. He could not run faster than them, but as fast—or nearly so.

The forest was dense. He ripped through it; leaped over rocks and ducked under branches. Shifting his eyes to the right, he saw two Up-Rivers coming in from the side. He veered to the left.

He came to a ridge with a sheer drop; stood for a moment, sucking in gasps of air. His heart was beating like a drum in his chest. Turning, he saw them coming upon him—could discern the wide, intent eyes of one as he rushed towards him, pulling his arm back to toss a spear. Fr. Massimo, in one fluid motion, tucked his head under his arms and threw himself off the ridge—rolled down the incline. He felt rocks thrust themselves into his back as he went and brush claw against his sides—and he bounced and then found his feet, leapt and bounded down, and then reaching the bottom, dove and flattened himself against the ground.

He bellied forward and along through the bushes, then rose to his feet and ran onward. By some miracle, he had not broken any bones—only scratched and bruised himself considerably.

He turned and gazed back. The incline he had tumbled down was more precarious than he had even thought and its height by no means small. At the top he could see several figures perched, looking down. It did not seem that they would attempt a descent, by that route in any case, but he did not stay to discover the truth of this. He turned and ran; ran on for hours, branches scratching his face and body, the muscles of his legs throbbing with pain, his chest hurting, and then finally collapsed, his breath coming in raw gasps. He took off his boots; his feet were sore, bleeding.

It was beyond mid-day and the forest was drenched in light. His body was exhausted, but his mind was alert. He closed his yes, listened; only heard a bird somewhere singing; and its song was trembling and zealous.

13

THE forest was close-packed, suffocating. Huge trees were strangled by vines, bandaged by moss. Birds screamed violently from high up branches on which trumpet flowers and orchids grew. Long centipedes could be seen crawling along the forest floor. Stands of giant ferns gave way to clumps of bamboo. There were flowers which smelled like rotting flesh and others that smelled like perfume. Strange sub-kingdoms of insects existed—big ugly beetles and strikingly beautiful cicadas. There were puddles of water in which leeches abounded and mosquitoes hummed through the air. Butterflies that looked like birds floated by and birds as bright as butterflies turned their heads back and opened their beaks as if thirsting for air.

The over-fertile soil spilled forth life of every description. Enormous Phantasmatodea crawled about on the foliage—walking sticks and brilliant green walking leaves—bug-eyed and alien-like. Emerald-coloured scarabs wrestled with golden bees and giant whistling spiders peered out from beneath tree roots and pear-coloured jumping spiders leaped from leaf to branch—some chaos of life, a swirling of short strokes cancelled by others long and flowing.

"There is nothing for it but to try and make my way back to Patntrm Village," he told himself.

He was hungry. Rooting about in a rotting tree trunk, he found long-horned beetle grubs and dined on them raw—a taste like squirming bone marrow. He got up and strolled forward; found a *ton* tree (Pometia pinnata) and ate its fruit. Darkness descended. A black placidity of moving volume. The priest slept in the open—it was not good sleep at all, blanketed by the sylvan cold and caressed with moisture. When he awoke, in the tangled light of dawn, he found an enormous rhinoceros beetle resting on his arm.

He flicked it away and sat up, his mind dark, memories stirred, and he remembered back to when he had been Father Xaverio Torturo—when he had been the Bishop of Rome, the very Vicar of Christ Upon Earth, the great Lando the Second. That was another life.

"How foolishly ambitious I was!" he thought.

Coming to West Papua, he had believed that he would be able to live a life of seclusion and charity—a life cultivating the inner mysteries of spirit, attempting to mitigate the appulse of evils done with good. But violence had followed him here too—had pursued him from life to life, and tested his charitable heart and revealed its frontiers.

But then he thought about his present situation and realised that, should he wish to survive, some ambition would be required.

The instinct for continued existence is, in man, possibly stronger than in any other species and it is doubtless this that makes us clothe ourselves, build walls and fences around our habitations and the altars at which we pray—for if we cannot help ourselves we ask the help of the choir of stars, of the thrones and the six-winged who know all triumphal hymns.

He got to his feet and walked.

Descending through a cloud forest, where ferns sprang up from the mossy ground and the trees grew like shrunken dwarfs—trunks distorted, branches bowing to the earth. To right and left small streams gurgled out pretty songs. Presently the terrain levelled off into a swampy stretch. A few branches lifted their heads to the sky, while others, as if for comfort, wrapped themselves around fellow branches, weeping on their kinsmen's arms. Webs of roots stretched themselves into the water. Bats the size of jackals flew through the air.

As he went along, it was impossible for him to progress on dry land alone and he was often compelled to wade through water, sometimes knee-deep, sometimes waist-high.

"At least here I am in no danger of running into any hostile people," he thought to himself, "for no humans could live in such a place."

But, not long after this thought, he suddenly glimpsed, from the corner of his eye, a human form through the brush. He looked closer, but it seemed to have been nothing more than a tree trunk, an optical illusion; and he continued, picking his way across a sort of isthmus as best he could. But then with certainty he saw a human standing in the water, and the latter slipped off noiselessly into the reeds.

"Then I was not mistaken," Fr. Massimo said, and continued his way; soon noticing five or six more of these people looking at him from the depths of the blades of green.

He stepped forward, said something to them, tried to communicate, and they quickly retreated into the greenery in alarm.

"Well, they appear not to be aggressive. So let my presence be seasoned with salt."

He sat on the bank and crossed his legs. Calmly he waited. Soon the autochthons began to slowly emerge once again. They stood at a distance, staring silently at him, their faces wearing expressions of blank curiosity. After about twenty minutes, one cautiously made his way forward—then backward—then forward again.

Fr. Massimo pointed towards his own stomach. "Hungry," he said.

The man stood, staring with curiosity at the bearded priest, who now pointed to his mouth.

"Food!"

The other blinked a few times, then looked down into the water, for a period standing still as stone, before suddenly snatching up a fish with remarkable dexterity. After breaking its neck, he set it on a rock about ten feet away from Fr. Massimo, but always kept himself at a distance, instinctively cautious.

The Italian took up the fish and ate rapidly, delighting in its raw, fresh taste. It was the first good food he had had in a long time and he could feel its nourishment enter into him and begin to strengthen him, and he thought of the mystic significance of the creature and the words Augustine had spoken about it and how Christ appeared to the Apostles on the shore of the Lake of Gennesaret.

The people were still standing, motionless, staring at him with intent interest.

He said thank you in West Bird's Head dialect, and the man who had given him the fish replied with a few words in a tongue he had never heard before—an odd language that sounded like the grating call of the crake. He detected a faint smile on the lips of his interlocutor, and smiled in return. The man slowly made his way forward, with motions darting, alert. He cocked his head to the left, blinked, straightened his body and then, with a gesture, invited Fr. Massimo to come to him.

The latter stepped into the water. The other stretched forward his hand and the priest grasped it. It was small, soft and friendly. The man began to lead him along, the others going before them. They waded through beds of swamp flowers, violet, beautiful, and then entered a malaleuca forest of dazzling green.

Fr. Massimo noticed that these people avidly avoided dry land, and seemed most at home wading through knee-deep water; and seeing their feet, which were large and flat, it seemed clear to him that they would suffer if they walked much the bare earth.

"These must be the Water-Bird People," he thought to himself, recalling Tokek's mention of them.

They were short, the tallest being not more than one hundred and fifty centimetres. Their legs were long and thin, and their torsos thick and somewhat stout. They were a shy people—frightened of everything, and their large, purplish eyes expressed sadness and alarm. The women showed a great modesty and when Fr. Massimo looked at them, they would lower their eyes.

After around an hour the party came to an islet of soggy ground from which soft vegetation grew. Small huts of grass rested on low stilts amidst the trees. The place had an impressive orderliness to it. There were grassy areas that seemed almost like manicured lawn.

The tribe was made up of only about forty or fifty individuals—and of these, very few were young. There were only around half a dozen children.

The inhabitants glared at the large priest with wonder and then, out of one of the dwellings, the headman crawled. He was a small man with a large mouth and kind eyes. He was old, probably at least seventy-five or eighty, and might well have been much older; with weathered features and a scant grey beard. His head was adorned with a few white feathers.

"*Buongiorno*," the priest said, instinctively.

The headman smiled, stood opposite Fr. Massimo staring up at his face and, to the great surprise of the latter, began to speak—not in the language he had heard the others use, but in an Italian of the purest quality; cadences of Dante mingling with Aretino— an assemblage of syllables that was like a meeting with old friends in some dream dimension.

"*Buongiorno*," he said. And then, continuing in Italian: "I am Po. This is my village and you are welcome here, though it might seem to you a doleful realm!"

Fr. Massimo Tetrazzini leaned forward in surprise, wondering if it was a hallucination.

"You are curious as to how I could know your language," Po observed. "I have the gift of the languages. Though little use it does me, oppressed as my people are by violent tribes on every side who have no wish to communicate. In the past it helped bring peace; and he who came before me gave it to me as it had been given to him; but now violence rules over men, for they can feel that the rocks are closing in on them."

He invited the priest to sit down on a nearby log and asked him about where he was from, what had brought him to that place, and Fr. Massimo, feeling greatly comforted by the sound of his own tongue, by being able to speak in his own language, related his adventures in as succinct a manner as possible.

"You were fortunate to escape from the Up-River tribe," Po said. "Many of my own people have suffered from them—have been carried off and devoured. And others have been murdered by the Tree People, who also have an appetite for human flesh. It seems the spirits of the forest reward cruelty, but pay no dividends on peace."

"It is the same throughout the world," Fr. Massimo stated. "Where I come from also, compassion is considered weakness and those who feast on their brothers prosper. Civilisation is indeed a somewhat meaningless word as man, by nature, whatever his condition, is brutal."

"You shall sleep here this night," Po said abruptly.

He waved his hand and a man brought Fr. Massimo a vessel of fresh, clean water, which was most welcome, and he was fed more fresh fish as well as some swamp taro and a serving of diplazium fern and then, after he had eaten his fill, pointed to an empty hut. The light of day was already weakening, he was tired, and so there he went. Within a thick bed of dried grass had been prepared for him. He lay down and thought of Po.

"If I were to murder this headman, and take his bright red pit, I would be facilitated with his gift of languages," he thought. "But to hurt him would make me a criminal of the lowest order." And he wondered how such reasoning could invade his mind; and with such thoughts he fell asleep quickly, but in his sleep he was walking, running, moving, looking for Sister Justina; a crowded maze of hallways lined with exotic potted plants, vines dangling from high ceilings, echoing questions being asked by those he could not see, and then he was presented with six weeping eyes as the tails of strange animals whisked about him sprinkling him with liquid as if they were numerous aspergillums.

He awoke just as the world was growing light; Po kneeling near him, pressing his shoulder.

"You must leave," the headman said.

"Now?"

"Very soon."

"But why?"

"Because you shall do away with my life, and will not want to stay. You will not be wanted here and your journey must continue."

Fr. Massimo was speechless. He almost wondered if he was not still asleep, still dreaming—or truly having a nightmare, for what Po said, if he understood him correctly, filled him with horror.

"My people will soon become extinct," he said. "Every man has his destiny. You must take my bright red pit—take it from my brain and ingest it."

The Italian sat up and shook his head.

"Our tribe is weak," the other said. "We are defenceless. Even this hut where we now sit was six months ago inhabited by a man named Palunen, who was snatched up and taken by the Tree People. And soon they or another people will come and exterminate the last of us. If you do not take it, another will. Take the pit, and my soul will go and join my ancestors, and hopefully you can use it for some purpose of greater good, for I see that you are a man travelling the path of the gods. During the night a being named Amazingly Elevated Flower came to me. His eyes were like stars and his mouth a lunar orb. We talked together. For long we talked together. It is not for me to repeat our discussion. There are intelligences which have such a strong perfume that only those without noses could be unaware of it. But I have decided."

Fr. Massimo grinned.

"But it takes two to decide such a thing."

"Yes. And you decided also. Did you not? It is just like this."

The headman climbed out of the hut. The priest sat for a moment, and then followed him. Po stood over by the log where the evening before they had sat. He stared at Fr. Massimo thoughtfully before pointing at the leftover food from the previous evening, some swamp taro and fish which sat on a leaf, saying:

"Take it."

The priest wrapped it up in the leaf and put it in his pocket.

"Come now," Po said, "let us walk a little."

The headman took the priest's hand and led him away from the village, through the marshy ground and through knee-high water to a rocky outcropping and there he sat and had the other sit near him.

"Go to the Tree People. Long ago their ancestor Het Diwai fell in love with a tree. He married her and they copulated together—and when she gave birth, it was to both trees and men. The brothers lived in the branches of their sisters; the sisters cloaked themselves in the leaves of their brothers. The headman there, whose name is Kembrur, has the power of fast walking. Take his kernel, his bright red pit, without hesitation, and you can move away all the more quickly. I am telling you this."

"Where do they live?"

"To the east of here, a half a day's strong walk. You will rise and fall, cross over a stream and be amongst very tall trees. But you must be careful, because Kembrur's people use arrows which they dip in a strong poison that they extract from the hooded pito-hui—that bad smelling bird that all other men avoid. If struck by one of their arrows, even if the wound is slight, your life is no longer your own."

Po fell silent. Fr. Massimo turned his gaze away. He did not know what to say, did not see how he could murder this old man, though he could not help desiring his ability, this ability of languages. And, as Po had indicated, he had thought of it the night before. But he was, after all, a man of God, and could not destroy another in order to enhance himself. Not that, in previous times, he wouldn't have performed such an act, but he had suffered much for that thirst for power and in this life wished to keep some purity to his actions.

"I cannot do this," he murmured.

The headman did not reply, and Fr. Massimo looked over. The former sat there, feet dangling in the water, eyes glassy, the lines of his mouth soft.

"Po," Fr. Massimo said. "Po!"

The other did not react; was unmoving. Fr. Massimo shook him, and he fell over.

Was he dead? The priest put his head to his chest, could hear a faint sound, feel a slight throbbing.

Fr. Massimo looked at his delicately drawn face and wondered if he should not try and revive the fellow, but then noticed a palpitation coming from his breast, which quickly grew more pronounced, until his chest cracked open, and his heart leaped out—leaped out of his body, out of an orange-red chasm in his chest, and jumped in the water, where it bobbed about a bit before sinking.

"His soul has flown from its cage," the priest said. Then, looking at the calm face of the headman: "If you have made this sacrifice, I can hardly refuse your gift."

He wet his lips with his tongue. His hands trembled as he reached for a rock. And then he cracked the other's skull open and dug within; some wet hot maze; and then he held it before his eyes, brilliant of colour, a ripened sardius, the tongue of a dragon's mouth, a pomegranate seed; his lips shut themselves around it.

A sweet flavour filled his mouth; his throat swallowed the strength of that strange nut. And he quietly wept.

14

F R. MASSIMO set off once again. His mind felt blank. He was far from happy with himself. He saw the world around him as one creature eating another—the small feeding on the large, the strong on the weak, the rich on the poor, and a bird in the hand was only better than two in the bush for the one with hands, but not for that with wings. The lines from Deuteronomy came to him in their original Hebrew:

"And thou shall eat the fruit of thine own body, the flesh of thy sons and of thy daughters."

And as he stepped through the marshy grass he was aware of a certain buoyancy in his mind, a certain well-oiled ease and the words that were floating through his head metamorphosed into others—the Hebrew words folding in their wings and becoming Ammonite and these in turn looped into the Balto-Slavic, into Lithuanian and Lettish. Then Latin twisted itself into Romanian before diving back into Persian and then wiggling away into Swedish—and the patterns of human language progress became clear and his mind was filled with light.

A bird shot up before him and flew into the sky.

An old song, one by Bartolino da Padova, came to him, and in a low voice he sang:

Alba columba con sua verde rama
in nobile zardino nutricata
pax, pax nunziando in su l'al' montata.

He reached the edge of the swampy area and began to ascend through the forest; grabbing hold of branches and pulling himself up, digging the toes of his boots into the earth, straining his thighs. He stood still and listened. The place was without sound. And on he went.

At a certain point an acrid smell accosted his nose. He noticed that the dirt was torn up as if some heavy animal had been rooting around.

He wondered if he was nearing the village of the Tree People, though it would seem he had not gone the distance mentioned by Po, and the landmarks were not there. But maybe this was the home of wild pigs? Proceeding, he came to a hollow of sorts.

The bark of the trees in the area was scraped away and the trees themselves were dead, six or eight human bodies hanging from their limbs. Flies buzzing about them, flesh swollen with maggots and an odious aroma haunting the air. The ground was covered with bones—broken skulls, femurs, ribs—the bones of men.

Fr. Massimo gazed about him, wondering what sort of animal lived in this place, and was just about

121

to walk on when he heard the sound of branches breaking, coming from the woods before him. He was about to turn to scramble back the way he had come, but then hesitated—suddenly entranced, made curious by the strange being he saw coming through the trees.

It moved along, dragging a corpse behind it; a lugubrious humming melody coming from its lips.

His arms were extraordinarily long, hanging down to the ground and his body was odd-shaped, muscular—it seemed almost as if it had been hewn out of wood, rolled in dirt and hair, shuffled through muck and compost. He had a huge mouth full of dripping yellow fangs that stretched across an almost perfectly round head. His eyes were small, and he squinted as if near-sighted.

He tied a vine around the wrist of the body and strung it up on a tree and then, moving amongst the other corpses, smelled and prodded each one, until, coming to one particularly decomposed and reasty, pulled it down.

Without noticing Fr. Massimo, he proceeded to devour the thing—first ripping open its bloated stomach and sucking out its rotten guts before tearing at the flesh, spitting out maggots, and sucking on the bones.

The priest was disgusted by the spectacle, but not frightened, for who did he have to fear but God?

"May my Lord go with me and may he not fail me or forsake me," he thought. "I must speak to this unhappy being and discover what tragedy he is afflicted by."

He stepped forward and approached the creature who at first did not notice him. But then looking, its eyes opened wide and its jaw fell, showing a mouthful of maroon-stained teeth.

"I am Massimo," the priest said in West Bird's Head.

The creature replied in a language the Italian had never heard before, what seemed to be an isolate with typological similarities to Puare, but he understood it perfectly. The magic of headman Po, the magic of the languages, gave him this power.

"Has another food bag come to me?"

"No. I am Massimo Tetrazzini."

"You speak my tongue."

"Yes."

"I am Gwanru."

"You are known."

"It is no wonder."

"You are a demon."

"A what?"

"A demon."

"You are a meal."

Fr. Massimo ignored the comment. He waved his hand around, gesturing towards the dead bodies.

"Why all this?"

"Why all what?"

"This destruction of life."

Gwanru took a bite of an arm, swallowed down the meat, rolled his eyes and then spoke:

"My people were first carved out of wood by the hands of the clouds. Long ago, forty or fifty generations, I was headman of the tribe. At that time we lived down in the valley, and were friendly with the birds and animals of the forest. They would come and, looking up at the sky, feed us—bringing us fruit, letting us drink from their mouths and eat their flesh. Pigs would rip open their own stomachs and offer us their entrails and bats would fly down our throats. My wives lay on their sides and grew fat. My sons swam in the rivers and grew strong. This is now some faraway dream. I have hollered at the gates of the underworld many times, asking to be reborn—as a lizard, a tree, anything—but always my requests are denied. I have leapt from cliffs and thrust my head into pools, but my life clings to my body like a vine to a tree. So I come and smell the blood they offer, or snatch someone from a village edge, and hang them up here in the trees until they ripen."

"Your story seems incomplete."

"I ate them."

"Who?"

"Everyone."

"Why?"

"As I grew old, I became afraid. In the forest I met someone. He had two shining eyes and a great many sharp teeth. He explained to me that by eating my people, I might extend my own life. And so when I returned, I proceeded to eat my wives, and when I had done with them, I ate my daughters and sons, and after I had completed this, my grandchildren and then all the rest of the people. I walk through the trees. If I see a man by himself, I take him and twist his neck. I am always hungry and can never get my fill!"

"And now?"

"Now, yes, I will have to kill you and let you cure," the demon said sorrowfully. "The only food I can digest is human flesh."

"But you must be tired of its taste."

"I cannot completely disagree. I want to join my ancestors who are eating sky-fruit, laughing and singing. Sometimes I can hear them—hear them calling my name. Sometimes it thunders and I hear them clap. My sons and the sons of my sons want me to join them. I do not want to forget them."

"Do not eat me," Fr. Massimo proposed, "and I will save your soul."

"Soul?"

"I will make it so that you can join your ancestors."

"How?"

"I am a man of God."

"Which god?"

"The one who created all things."

"You know her?"

"Yes."

The demon grinned awfully. "I think you are lying," it said. "A long time ago a black pond spilled out of her loins and the stars grew there. She is silent and does not care. When she gets hungry she will eat everything. Moving, jumping things like you and I bore this woman. How could you know her?"

"Because her son, Jesus Christ of Nazarene, came and died for my sins."

125

"Sins?" the demon said, opening his eyes wide.

"Eating human flesh is a sin. These sins pile up and tie you down to evil existences. I will plead God to show you mercy so that you can join your ancestors—so that you can pass into a more perfect state, shedding your earthly appetites and concerns. You will have one meal less now, but will eat good things in the land beyond for eternity and will be cooled by the ceaselessly fanning wings of the seraphim."

Gwanru cocked his head to one side and seemed thoughtful for a moment.

"If it is so, then it would be good. And if not . . ." Then, with a sigh: "Go. I have enough flesh here for the time being. I pick life from the peripheries of the villages and it is offered by those weaker than myself, by those who do not remember as I do. You are likely lying, as men do, but you are an excellent liar and you have spoken with me in my tongue—and how you learned that I do not know—but it has pleased me to speak after so long being silent. So, yes, go, and go quickly, before I change my mind."

And so Fr. Massimo left, walked away through the forest, the stench of the place still clinging to his nostrils

15

DOM RAMIRO was alone. His eyes sat lost in blue circles. His facial hair had grown out—forming an ugly, unkempt beard in which small insects lived, loved with great fury, and died, and the hair on his head flared up in wild profusion. The Up-Rivers saw that while Fr. Massimo had gone, Dom Ramiro had stayed. They saw that he ate flesh with a greater joy than even themselves.

"He is possessed of some kind of spirit," they said one to another.

They saw no use in keeping him jailed, for since he had not run when given the chance, he would not run. The cage door was left open. He wandered about the village, set his buttocks down in the dust. When he was given meat, he ate it; when given bones, he chewed them.

He felt as if he had arrived home after a long voyage—because probably his ancestors, even in faraway Europe, had put their teeth marks on the thigh-bones of their enemies, or friends. Yes, humans by nature were cannibals. Some ate the flesh or brains of those

127

they caught in battle while others, much more brutally, cannibalised on their brothers' labour, freedom, happiness—mankind being more savage than any jungle cat, more rude than any crawling bug, more viperous than any slithering serpent.

These were not the thoughts that passed through Dom Ramiro's mind, but the reality that he felt. He had always been primitive. Before he had been covered with a cassock, perfumed with toilet soap. Now he stood naked, smelling of old blood. It could no more be said that he had regressed than that he had advanced. The technological progression that modern man prides himself on is simply the retroactive genius of those who came long before. The leap from caveman to bureaucrat, aborigine to prelate or dignified priest, is a much smaller one than most people think. It is simply a matter of the broth cooking a little longer—but a hot broth can cool with as much ease as a cool broth be made hot.

"I do not understand this man," said Saragigi.

"He has power," Owarbwa replied.

"But what power? I see no magic."

Owarbwa shrugged his shoulders. "The power of universal hunger."

"I shall eat his brains and see what I can find."

"Let us wait until the moon slumbers and then we will give him to Gwanru. You could wade through his brains for fifty days and fifty nights and find nothing more than small worms. And if we are to speak the truth, to look at him inspires me not with hunger."

Saragigi nodded his head in agreement. "Yes," he said. "We shall give him to Gwanru—for then it will be one less of our own that he snatches away."

If homicide is the tendency towards madness, cannibalism is madness itself and it is most certain that the effects of killing one's neighbour, of eating one's fellow species, would not be unlike that of a strong stimulant. A rat, once it has tasted its fellow's flesh, gains in ferocity tenfold. Cruelty stretches the nerves taut—makes men go to war, kidnap their neighbours—all in the need to continue to nourish themselves on the flesh of their own species. If mankind can dare call hunting a sport, why should it not call anthropophatic murder a pleasure?

The priest from Portugal, no longer caged, felt a violent need for physical exercise and galloped through the meadows. When he came to a tree, he pulled himself into its braches and leaped from one to the next. He took rocks and hurled them about; flung himself on the pole in the middle of the village and climbed half way up it, then leaped down. He grabbed up a bone and cracked it between his teeth and sucked from it the marrow.

The woman who had stood by the cage staring at him now came.

"I am Mbalnga," she said. "I am Mbalnga and you shall be my husband."

He did not understand what she said.

She lifted her tree bark fibre veil, revealing a delicately drawn face, sharp eyes. She took his hand, brought it to her mouth, and sucked on one of his fingers.

And beneath the wings of her shelter the two bodies absorbed the dirt. They gnawed at eachother's ears like soldiers with their arms cut off, desperate to inflict damage with their tongues and teeth in tameless chivalry. The priest, who had been, as was proper, a virgin of sorts, lost himself in her florid spasms, which were like the blue juice of shadows bleeding at dawn. The restraint he had attempted to practice from his youth was swept away like a twig in a rapid river, and the instinct of lust, like the instinct for survival, for murder, made him wriggle and quake with convulsive pleasure.

The waxing crescent crawled to the first quarter, and the waxing gibbous began to gather up light—and on a day the sun rose bright and some warriors came along in the late morning with two victims that they had snatched from some nearby tribe, and Saragigi gave instructions for one of them to be slaughtered for his lunch and when this was done and the flesh was cooked he sat with it cut up before him, the entire village staring on hungrily while the headman casually ate, filled his mouth with carnage.

Dom Ramiro approached, was attracted by the sight of the other's jaws, by that vital consommé dripping down his chin, by the colour of the meat.

He licked his lips and stretched out his hand.

"Wait for my scraps, which are even too good for one like you."

The priest blinked his eyes. He did not understand. Reaching for the meat, his hand was slapped away. He reached again and Saragigi thrust his foot in his face.

The villagers laughed. Dom Ramiro saw the food, saw that he could not have it, and felt a roar fill his head. Mortiferous stars veiled his vision and he sprang at the other, latched his teeth onto his throat and bit deep. Saragigi dropped his meal, sprang to his feet, danced around, trying to pull the priest off of him—beating him, thrusting his knee into him.

The Up-Rivers gathered around shouting, but none of them lent Saragigi assistance. The strange fury of the priest both startled and interested them.

Finally Dom Ramiro unlatched himself. Blood spurted wildly from Saragigi's neck. He fell to the ground, clutching at the wound. The Portuguese slipped near him, kneeling, pushed the weakening hands aside and began to suck away at the headman's blood while the latter's bulging eyes shifted over, watching this vampire at work.

Eventually, almost bloated with blood, Dom Ramiro pulled away his empurpled mouth and wiped it with the back of his hand. He looked down and blinked. Saragigi lay dead.

Mbalnga picked up a piece of firewood and battered his head in, then joyously poked about in his brain, and, extracting the red kernel, offered it to Dom Ramiro, who swallowed it down and then proceeded, with great satisfaction, to gorge himself on the brain.

The villagers devoured the body of the headman in a macabre celebration. And so it is that whatever awe or fear he had inspired in the others, whatever respect, was forgotten the moment they saw his blood, saw him lifeless.

Later, when darkness fell, Dom Ramiro shone a light out of his back to the delight of all and after, it seemed as if Saragigi's flesh had acted as an aphrodisiac and Dom Ramiro and Mbalnga were like two larvae feeding on each other.

The evening wolf obeys only the marrow of bones; the famished lion finds the vulture more beautiful than the sun.

The Up-River People saw in Dom Ramiro a being deserving of something more than respect. The women came and gave him offerings of roasted beetles and grilled rodents; the warriors bowed before him before they went off on a raiding expedition and when they returned with a fresh victim, they offered him the choicest delicacies. At night they submitted young women of the tribe to him and, intoxicated on carnage, he smothered them with his blood-stained lips, his priestly vows long forgotten, only Christ remaining in his mind, nailed to a cross, offering his flesh for raw consumption—an eternal repast of warm sweating meat.

He had graduated from the state of prisoner, from being a celibate encaged, but was, however, not precisely headman to the tribe—being rather treated as some deity, some embodiment of base instincts, an avatar of universal appetency. He seemed incapable of learning even the most rudimentary elements of their language, and was only able to pronounce a few words, such as "eat," "drink" and "flesh".

16

FR. MASSIMO, having left Gwanru, climbed up the hill and then descended.

"Po told me to go to the village of the Tree People. The chief of that tribe has the power of fast walking. If I could only gain that ability . . ."

Forests and mountains, seemingly endless; and he came to a stream which sang pleasantly.

He kneeled down, drank from it, and then stepped over its waters.

He had to find his way home. But to do so he had to turn assailant—to do what was not in the domain of a man of God to do. So then was he a man of God as he professed? St. George had killed a dragon, yes, but only in order to save the maidens of Silene. But then, had not the Archangel Michael given St. Mercurius a magical sword with which to slay men and had not St. Nuno Álvares Pereira achieved victory in war by having the name of the Blessed Virgin inscribed on his own blade?

If God had created the world, then had he not created violence too? For though He commanded man not to kill, saying that it was for Him to kill and make alive, yet also it was said by the son of David that to all things there was a season, and in a certain season one might need to heal, while in another one might need to take a life.

A grim smile curled his lips, for he recalled that, in past times, he would not have needed quite so much sophism to perform such a sanguinary deed.

Forward Fr. Massimo went and presently heard the light sound of human voices. Two men carrying bows and arrows were walking through a meadow. They were tall, with thin, wiry limbs. They wore penis sheaths and necklaces of bones. The priest followed them at a distance as they passed into the forest. For a period he could see them ahead of him, and then they disappeared. The only sound was that of birds calling in the distance. He walked onward and presently came to a grove of immensely tall trees. He looked up. They were leafless, and high in their braches huts were built; a village, on platforms, accessible by notched poles near which vines hung which acted as banisters.

Fr. Massimo stood thoughtful for a period.

"I am poured out like water," he thought, "and all my bones are out of joint. My heart is like wax: it is melted in the midst of my bowels."

He approached the base of a tree and called out. Silence. Again he opened his mouth and let sound come forth.

A voice from up high said: "Who are you?"

Due to his language magic, the priest understood with clarity.

"A friend," he cried out.

"How can we tell?"

"I carry no weapon. I come alone."

"For what reason are you here?'

"To speak with your headman, Kembrur."

Silence.

"I have things to tell Kembrur!"

Silence.

Fr. Massimo sat on the ground, cocked his head up, and stared at the treetops, the platforms—half expecting that at any moment some object would be hurled at him, at his apparent challenge.

"Go away," a voice said presently—a voice different from the first.

"No!"

There was silence.

"If these are cannibals, they are of a rather timid variety," Fr. Massimo thought.

"Go away," came the voice again.

"Let me speak with Kembrur!"

After a brief period, a figure showed itself and made its way about ten metres down the notched pole.

"I am the strongman!"

The man was rather tall, with a thick torso and long legs. He had very large eyes which were half shaded by their drooping lids.

"You are Kembrur?" the priest asked, rising to his feet.

"Yes, I am the strongman, Kembrur."

"And I am Massimo."

"You came from the land of shadows?"

"This could be."

"What do you want?"

"To speak with you."

"You are speaking."

"Come down and let us talk face to face. I have many things to say."

"No. You are a demon."

"I am a man."

"Your skin is too strange for it to be that of a man. You are a demon."

And with that the headman climbed back up the notched pole.

Fr. Massimo stood looking up at the tree and was wondering what course to take when an arrow whistled by his ear and stuck in the earth near him. He remembered Po's words, about these darts being imbued with a deadly poison, and put distance between himself and the tree houses, making his way back into the woods.

The tree village was at such a height that they could surely monitor him from a great distance, so he walked and walked and made his way over a hill. He took out the swamp taro and fish and ate, then lay down and rested. Darkness fell and in the darkness he quietly made his way back, hiding himself in the woods near the village. High up, the tree houses were aglow with the cooking fires they made up there.

He sat with his back against a tree and waited.

It was no situation of comfort. The air became chilly, his belly grew hungry again. He wished he had some prosciutto to eat, a cigarette to smoke, a bottle of wine to drink, wondered if he would ever drink one again—wine of Veneto—where he had come from, both in this incarnation and the previous. The previous—with its brilliance and suffering—an existence he had been eager to move beyond.

When he had first come to West Papua, he had been delighted. To be away from the noise of Italy and the machinations of priests, to be surrounded by the grandeur of nature, had been a wonderful thing. He had thought it not impossible that he might even spend the rest of his days cultivating himself and lending assistance to the Patntrms. But now, looking up at the moon, he could not help the longing he suddenly felt for Europe.

"Even as the soul migrates from body to body, it carries with it the tinctures of the past," he murmured to himself. "And though the actors might change their masks and roles, they are attracted to those stages where they had most success."

That he was where he was in order to kill Kembrur he knew, accepted. But he had not formulated any concrete plan. His first thought had been to win the trust of the Tree People, but this had clearly failed, and so his next idea was one of ambuscade.

The night kept watch and then sealed its eyes as the sun reached up, and light came.

He watched the tree houses. A woman descended from one, went into the forest and then returned, climbing back to the great heights. The sound of human voices came from up there. A shout—a sort of whoop. And another, and another. Men climbed down from several of the tree houses and formed a group, a group of five in all, with the headman among them. They all carried bows and arrows, except Kembrur, who carried a long-handled stone-headed axe.

They walked towards Fr. Massimo; were within forty feet of him, but did not see him, and passed by.

"I will kill a tree-kangaroo today," he heard one of the men say.

"I would rather slay a man and lunch on his heart."

"Every day cannot be a day of good feast."

The priest rose up, and with a careful gait, followed carrying his boots in his hands.

After proceeding for about twenty minutes, two of the men wandered off in one direction, leaving the headman with two others, who proceeded in an easterly direction.

They went slowly, stalking forward, looking for game—and Fr. Massimo had to practice the utmost caution in order not to be seen or heard—staying far behind, moving barefoot and stepping with delicate precision.

One of the men pointed. Up ahead was a young cassowary. He pulled back his bow and let an arrow fly. The bird cried out in pain, a frightening, storm-like roar, and darted off into the trees, with the arrow lodged in its side.

"It is hit!"

"But not dead."

"Go run after it," said the headman. "I will wait. For me to catch this animal is too simple of a task, for at no great pace does it run. You two must exercise your shanks."

The two men ran after it while Kembrur waited, standing still, leaning on his axe and looking after them.

Fr. Massimo lost no time in making his move. He set down his boots and ran forward. Kembrur turned his head, a surprised expression on his face as the priest ploughed his fist into it, crushing the nose of the headman, who staggered back, stunned, as blood began to adorn his features.

The axe had fallen to the ground and Fr. Massimo moved for it, but Kembrur, recovering himself, threw his body forward, clawing desperately at the priest.

Fr. Massimo knifed his fist into the other's side. The headman swung one of his legs around those of the Italian, tripping him, throwing him down. Kembrur, driven by both anger and fear, kicked at him and then stabbed at his face with his heel, but the priest rolled over and sprang to his feet only to be immediately assaulted by the hot slapping hands of the other, which felt like hurled rocks. Fr. Massimo got in as many body hits as he could while pulling his head back and out of the way. The headman, however, lunged forward and got in a few good blows to the mouth, cheeks and chin.

The priest realised that he had little time to do away with his adversary, for soon enough the hunters would return, and if he was able to hold his own against one man, he was certainly no match for three or five.

He made a feint with his left that deceived the headman and then delivered a long, powerful blow with his right to the chin that sent his opponent toppling back to the ground. Fr. Massimo sprang on him. Both men were wet with blood, and rolled about, chest stuck to chest, hugging close. Kembrur, whose mouth was frothing with saliva, had had the worse of it, and swung and struggled desperately, his eyes glazed with confusion.

The priest worked his way behind him, swung his arm around his neck and pulled back fiercely.

He heard a loud cracking sound. Kembrur let out a spasm and went limp. Fr. Massimo held him tightly for a moment, before realizing that he was dead.

The priest freed himself from underneath the body, took up the nearby axe and, lifting it high, brought it down with as much force as he was able and the skull cracked like the shell of a boiled egg. He brought the axe down several more times until he was able to dislodge a piece of cranium from the mashed scalp.

Then, reaching inside the brain, he pulled out the red pit and, putting it in his mouth, proceeded to ingest it. Unlike that of Po, however, it had a bitter, foul taste, and the priest had difficulty to keep from vomiting and, just when he had got it down, the sound of the returning hunters came to him and he thrust himself into the forest, grabbed up his boots, feeling a certain loathing for himself, a gloomy emptiness.

"The ego is indeed harder than any rock and stronger than any steel," he thought.

He moved through the forest quietly for a spell, then sat down on a log and put on his boots. Wiping his mouth with the back of his hand, he realised that he had been salivating heavily. He rose to his feet and jogged on, feeling a trembling about him; stumbled into the meadow where he had first seen the Tree People and stood, legs apart, ears alert, in the sun, letting its warmth wash over his punished body.

He heard shouts behind him. The hunters were tracking him—surely had every intention of killing him, of avenging their perished leader. He began to run, to thrust one leg in front of the next; felt a sudden elasticity in them. Stretching them out, it seemed that they lunged forward a great distance, were almost made of liquid instead of flesh and bone. He found that, with but little effort, they moved with great rapidity.

"The fast walking," he thought. "With this I shall easily elude my pursuers."

He found himself dashing through the forest, leaping over fallen trees, fording rivers at a bound—moving at great speed as if in a dream, trees and hills rushing by him. The Tree People pursued him, but the priest easily outdistanced them. He felt as if he were in some childish dream—an athlete, a superman. The moth cannot fathom the speed of the swallow, and the swallow, given the wings of an eagle, becomes a magic bird.

He stopped for a moment to catch his breath, but found that he was not in the least tired.

"Like some gift from Mephistopheles," he thought to himself—but thought without compunction as he proceeded onward, exhilarated by this new sorcery.

17

THE sound of swift motion filled his ears. He forgot his cuts and bruises and enjoyed his new-found power of locomotion. The area covered in the hour that followed was great and he moved his legs with avidity, thrilled with the speed of their gesture.

It is certainly true that the visible aspects of the universe are few when compared to the invisible and Fr. Massimo could not help but think that God was drunk, having cast into being not only marvels vegetable and mineral, but also those of odylic force and mystic ability, and drew men on by subtle threads, lending them power and taking it away, lending them life and taking it away, in some unapproachable order that so greatly resembled chaos.

To move amongst the trees took a certain amount of concentration. He leapt over a brook, then through an area of high reeds, then through a grass plain and up a steep slope.

He reached the top of a ridge, acute and rocky, and saw in the distance smoke rising out of the forest and

then, looking more closely, could make out habitations. He descended, neared the place with caution—
drawn forward by curiosity, by the natural instinct in
man to observe other men—an instinct which might
well be the cause of much of the world's evils, since
bad things come from association much more often
than solitude, from men seeing men, convening with
them, sharing glances or opinions, despising or desiring. For the instinct in mankind makes them wish
to at once move in flocks and herds and to be the
predator, who picks off the stray animal from the parade and slaughters it and eats of its flesh. And so it
is that a smiling, joke-loving man at a cocktail party
might, when the party is done, haunt the alleys with
a knife or strangecord in hand, or a loving husband
and father, thrust into uniform, order a firing squad to
destroy some fellow humans pushed up against a wall.

The land rose up again, and he found himself on a
smaller hill, just overlooking the place.

The village consisted of three tremendous long
houses. In front of each was a large totem of sorts—
one in a humanoid shape, the features of which were
nothing but a pair of eyes and a gaping mouth—another appearing to be a sort of placental mammal—
the third an ominous bird with four wings and two
beaks, one on its head, the other its belly.

Several women were vigorously at work about the
place, carrying water, gathering in wood, while a few
men stood about leaning on spears of great length, five
metres or more. Another man, unarmed, appeared to

have pieces of rotting flesh dangling from his arms and this fellow was seated, carving a piece of wood and chanting:

> Idoai, Idoai
> Come home
> And guide us
> To where
> The meat is sweet

"This must be the village of the Ubuhae Folk," Fr. Massimo reasoned.

He recalled the words of Tokek, who had said that the headman of this place, Idoai, had the ability to go to the underworld.

"I could do as I did with Kembrur," Fr. Massimo thought. "But why should I not let him keep this ability? For it is not to the underworld that I wish to go, but to the higher planes and of killing I have had enough for the present."

18

THE priest set off into the forest, towards the south.

He went for some distance and then, when darkness came, spent the night at the edge of a glade.

The next day he went on; found a narrow and somewhat precarious way that led over the mountains and then with his magic strides descended.

He saw a range of hills in the distance, at least seven or eight kilometres away. A half an hour later, he was climbing over them. He glided over grassy highlands and leaped down rocky slopes—glorious views fleeting by his vision.

Presently familiar objects came into sight—the shape of well-known hills.

He stopped for some moments and observed the skyline in the distance.

"I am not too far from home," he murmured to himself with satisfaction.

He urged himself onward. The ground flew beneath his feet. He went up and down hills with the greatest of ease and presently, in the early hours of evening, found himself on Bad Mountain, between Patntrm Village and the Awi village, before the cave he had been at not long since with Dom Ramiro. Now the sun had said goodbye to the earth and darkness was laying herself over the land.

He was but a short distance to Patntrm Village. What normally would take him a couple of hours to walk, but with the fast walking would but take him fifteen or twenty minutes. But descending the hill in the dark would be unsafe, so he determined to camp out there and then finish his journey the next morning.

He sat down on a rock and recited the *Beatus vir*.

The sky was clear, appearing like a vast black sheet pierced with pin holes.

He looked up and wondered about Dom Ramiro, if he were dead or alive, and wondered how much, or how little, of his fate he should reveal to the Church authorities. Was it still possible for the Portuguese to be rescued? Would the Pontifical Mission Guild even desire him back—a man who was reduced to eating the flesh of his fellow men?

While his mind was thus turning, he heard the sound of softly laid steps coming from the direction of the cave, and from there a figure emerged—a dark shadow that stalked forward, passed him, and then returned, stopped not far from Fr. Massimo and stood still there before him, outlined against the night sky—a masculine shape, with some living thing, some animal, moving about on its shoulder. For what seemed like a long period the priest was not entirely sure if he was aware of his presence or not, until he spoke.

"Who are you?" he asked.

"I might ask the same."

"No one comes here after dark."

"You are here."

"Yes. But darkness is to me as light is to other men, just as bitterness is to me as sweetness is to others, for I was born in my own way."

The man's voice was remarkably deep, and seemed the voice of one who was at once intelligent and wolf-like, relentless and subdolous—a snarling growl from eager jaws.

The priest introduced himself.

"I live in Patntrm Village," he said.

"But you are certainly not Patntrm!"

"No."

"Where is the place of your birth?"

"Far away."

"But you live in Patntrm Village?"

"Yes."

"So that is how it is!" A flash of white teeth could be seen in the darkness. "I have long thought of . . . paying it a visit."

"Your name?"

"I am Idoai."

"Headman of the Ubuhae Folk?"

"Not without some fame!"

The creature on his shoulder let out a snickering sound.

"And that?" Fr. Massimo asked.

"This is Kib, my assistant, my advisor, and my constant companion."

"You have come from the cave?"

"From the underwold. Every three or four moons I go below to visit the wives I have there and bring them flowers. The wives I have up here are unable to give me joy, since they are not yet demons and are amateurs in the art of salacious gratification."

"You are able to pass to the underworld unhindered?" Fr. Massimo asked.

"Yes, it is my power. Just as you too have some power."

Fr. Massimo did not reply.

"You speak the languages," Idoai said.

"I understand you."

"Your skin is that of a ghost. I am looking at your eyes. They seem shallow and moss-tinted."

"It is dark, but you can see me?"

"Yes. You can speak, and I can see so well."

The little thing whispered something in Idoai's ear and once again Fr. Massimo could see that flash of teeth, evidence of a smile.

"Let us eat," Idoai then said to Fr. Massimo. "The night is long. Let us eat and converse together, for we each have things to say and to hear."

"I have no food."

"Do your hunting Kib," the headman of the Ubuhae Folk said to the little demon and the latter sprang off his shoulder and away, disappearing into the night with an unpleasant tittering sound.

Idoai took up some dried leaves and two sticks and rubbed one against the next and out of them a flame leaped. He added sticks of wood and then larger pieces, and a fire was soon built and the Italian could then see what his companion of the moment was like. His features were finely drawn, eyes alert. Around his neck hung a necklace of human teeth. Though he was by no means young, his body was well formed, muscular, with an athletic suppleness to it.

Presently Kib reappeared, came up to the fire circle, and Fr. Massimo could also observe the creature. It had large eyes and a snub nose and a grinning little mouth—looked something like a cross between a bat and a small, unpleasant looking child. It now carried a number of diminutive and dead animals tied together by their tales—marsupial shrews and brush-tailed rabbit rats, speckled dasyures and bandicoots. Idoai skewered them on sticks and began to roast them, leaving a few aside for Kib, who ate them raw—his eyes constantly darting up to meet those of the priest.

"And where were you born?" Idoai asked.

"In the wilderness it seems," the priest replied.

"The wilderness?"

"A place of fiery serpents and scorpions."

Idoai handed Fr. Massimo a skewer and the men began to eat. The headman laughed and nodded his head as he ate.

"The food is good."

"Yes."

The small roasted animals were by no means delicious, but Fr. Massimo was hungry and ate. He felt that the man opposite him was indeed far above the average. He had a certain strange charisma that both attracted and startled the priest. When he looked over, the man smiled, but Fr. Massimo could not answer that smile with his own, for he had no trust.

Idoai took another skewer of meat from the fire and handed it to Fr. Massimo, but as the latter reached for it, the former dropped it. The priest stretched forward and was just grabbing it when there was a clap of thunder.

Flaming hands reached out and pulled his head to the ground. Something sailed into his side and he felt a lancing pain. Through a red mist, he saw a flutter of movement. There was a sort of chuckling sound and his mind clicked into place as he saw Idoai's foot swoop down and kick him in the chest.

The Italian winced and cried out.

His hand still grasped the skewer.

He saw Idoai's face floating in front of him and then he triggered some spring in his arm and his fist lunged forward and a scream lunged towards his ears.

The little demon was biting into his arm. He grabbed it and tore it away, then dashed it against the rocks. The creature let out a squeal of pain, then, half-broken, began to crawl away. Fr. Massimo took the stick and approached it. The animal looked over its shoulder with eyes that were at once pleading and mean and the priest beat it dead.

He straightened himself up. Idoai was lying before him. He did not move. The skewer had run through his right eye, deep into his brain. The light from the fire danced on his face and body.

Fr. Massimo kneeled near him. His breath was short. His left eye blinked. And soon he lay a corpse.

Fr. Massimo clenched his fists.

"The underworld," he murmured. "Is God then angry every day? Is my spiritual development then so closely aligned with suffering? Ah, well, my destiny . . ."

He bent over and picked up a heavy stone, stepped up to the corpse. And he proceeded to disgorge the bright red pit from Idoai's head—to nibble it down like some type of horrible dessert and the darkness grew clear.

19

WHEN FR. MASSIMO arrived back to Patntrm Village, it was early morning. The light was new and still dull. A silence hung about the place. He could hear a baby crying in one of the huts. Vali was seated on the steps of the primitive church, his head hung low. When the priest approached, the young man looked up, his eyes red, his face a desert—the face of one who had not slept that night—a face without joy or appetition, as if his youth had been thrown away and his mouth had forgotten how to smile.

"You are back."

"Yes."

"We thought you were dead."

"I am not."

Fr. Massimo frowned. He had expected to be greeted with more enthusiasm.

"Something is not right," he said.

"That is so."

"Tell me."

"Sister Justina," Vali said.

"Where is she?"

"While you were gone three women came down with the sickness. Sister Justina administered to them all, uselessly. Then last night . . ."

"Yes?"

Vali shook his head.

"What happened?" Fr. Massimo asked in a strained voice.

"It was her turn."

"Her turn?'

"You must help her."

Fr. Massimo suddenly understood and rushed to her hut and Vali followed him. Two women were attending her. When they saw the priest, they turned their eyes to the ground.

"She has the sickness," one of them said.

Sister Justina lay on her bed. Her eyes were closed and her lips were white and dry. A shiver ran through her body, which at that moment looked excessively delicate, frail; a wounded butterfly being carried away by the wind.

The priest shook her, talked to her. Her eyes opened and wandered, lost in some other world, her consciousness being pulled away. She did not seem to see or recognise him and the only words out of her mouth were some vague reference to clerical rank and the contemplation of sacred things. He took her hand. It was without warmth and did not respond to his touch.

The priest had tried to cure women of this before her, and failed.

"What can I do?" he thought. "What is my knowledge good for? Is the only thing left then . . . my religion?"

His religion. Faith. Others had claimed it in order to perform miraculous deeds, miracles, why not he? Was it so naïve to expect some help from forces unseen—those powers which made rivers rush and stars gleam and filled men with wonder?

He fell to his knees and prayed.

"Most Loving Jesus," he said in a loud and sonorous voice, "for our salvation you performed the painful journey of the cross and for us your sinews were torn and veins were opened and your sacred body poured forth blood. Now the thorns of life have fallen on the head of this woman who lies before me, Sister Justina Monticelli, who, while others have done evil, has done but good—this woman in whose heart you are entombed. Jesus Christ crucified have mercy on her. Eternal Father have mercy on her. Save her from the shipwreck of this current affliction as you did save Noah from the Universal Deluge. Rainbow of peace, Queen of Virgins, open up your maternal heart for this woman. Ora pro nobis, virgo dolorosissima. Dominis ad adjuvand un me festina."

But not all that is asked for is received. It is said that one must have confidence in God for Him to grant one's prayers. Had Fr. Massimo such confidence? Did he have full faith in divine mercy? Did the god that he prayed to exist, and if he did was the request of the Italian priest agreeable to his will? Whatever the case, his pious ejaculations, his prayers, were ineffective as were other measures he took and by early afternoon she had died. The women who had stood by her began weeping and beating their breasts.

Tears fell from Vali's eyes.

Fr. Massimo stood still, some object made of stone, his own eyes hard and dull.

In his previous incarnation, as Fr. Xaverio Torturo, this woman had helped him; had fed him and read to him from the Holy Bible and had done her best to relieve his suffering. She had come to West Papua by his will and, because of this, was no more. He shook his head. He could not accept such a situation and for him the logic of what to do was simple.

"Guard her body," he told Vali. "Do not let anyone touch it. Do not let anyone go near her!"

He left the room and went to his own hut. There was a mirror and within its frame he saw a bearded face, a gaze of grave tranquillity amidst cuts and bruises. He let his tattered garments fall to the ground and sponge bathed his body which looked like the body of one who had been tortured. Naked, he shaved his chin and washed his face.

His eyes strayed over his library, and then to his medicine chest. He reached within, took out a phial of spikenard oil, and with it anointed his body. The room filled with its aroma and he thought of Mary who had given the ointment to Jesus, and the complaints against her—and he wondered at the confusion, for Mark said it was the head that was anointed, while John said it was the feet—but in any case it revived his flesh and lent him consecration.

155

He put on a fresh cassock and a pair of less worn boots; drank abundantly of fresh water; slowly and thoughtfully smoked a cigarette; and then, without accompaniment, set off up the mountain. Using the fast walking, it was only a matter of a quarter hour before he achieved the summit, and in a few more minutes he was at the opening of the cave.

The body of Idoai was lying near the cold fire, eyes and mouth open in stunned absence, head open in coagulated blood. Flies now buzzed about it. Soon animals would come and eat it.

"At least his soul was here at the cave opening," Fr. Massimo thought, "and did not need to travel far—or did he? For what is the distance to hell?"

And then he looked at the form of the demon, shattered and insignificant with ants already crawling over it.

Fr. Massimo turned towards the cave. The fetishes stared at him—their mouths seemed almost to be speaking, to be humming some tune of fear and warning—a silent treble that shrugged and nudged its slippery hazard.

He entered.

The place was dark, but, due to having eaten Idoai's bright red pit, he could see—not with the clarity of day, but as if looking at a day-lit world through a somewhat blurry lens. He walked forward. At first the way was constricted—bats hung from the ceiling and spiders clung to their star-shaped nets. There was a smell of dead animals and a layer of small bones covered the ground. Gradually the cavern broadened out, a steep descent opened up. A narrow path lay to one side, while to the other there was a sheer drop. Fr. Massimo proceeded, walking quickly but cautiously. A deep, boisterous laughter came from somewhere, but he ignored it. There was a sound like waves breaking on the shore, but he paid it no mind.

Then the drop to one side disappeared and the path grew broad, and though always descending, relatively straight. As he went, subtle ghosts glided past him and strange bony white creatures like large phantom Armadillidium bustled around his feet. Now and again sparkles of green light flitted about the walls.

A strange intoxication seemed to grab hold of his sight. At one point he fancied he was walking by the shore of a lake around which horses were feeding on long and tender grass; at another he seemed to be gliding through a neighbourhood of grand houses in the windows of which he could see people fornicating, seeming to be engaged in the most intense pleasure. And then the visions would fade, and on either side there were just moist walls of rock.

"So you destroyed me, sealed me off from the mountains and forests, but soon my demon wives will embrace my soul."

The distance to wherever this tunnel led was great, for despite the fast walking his progress seemed slow and stunted. He walked for what surely was a great many hours, his cassock sweeping along the slimy walls, his gaze steadfast in front of him. At one point he passed by a crowd of naked, fat men with blue skin beating on drums while others danced wildly about them. At another the way lay near a river of larvae which seethed beside him—thrashing in waves of soft slithering fat—and further on he felt something licking at his heels, but each time he turned around the animal, some long, swift thing, darted off and hid in the darkness.

He went on in haste, his fast-moving feet rushing over the stones and blue earth.

"Something—something for my hunger!"

He looked over. A being was standing near him with its hand outstretched. The fellow was naked and had fragile looking legs and considerable feet. His stomach was like a huge drum—it seemed the belly of a rhinoceros or elephant. His head, which seemed to float above his body, was absurd, with large ears and eyes that looked like onions. Indeed the head seemed to exist apart, to be not even joined to the body—and only held in place by the creature itself, who grasped its left ear with one hand as one might the handle of a jar. But, looking closely, Fr. Massimo noticed that there was indeed a neck—a neck of extreme subtlety, of no more thickness than a needle—a long wiry fibre that connected the head to the trunk.

"Food," the creature murmured. "Please, some food for the hungry."

But Fr. Massimo had nothing to give; and so, sadly, he continued on his way.

As he descended, a slight red mist began to appear, creeping along the earth, a wisp occasionally struggling upward, fluttering about his waist, drifting up to his throat. The air became suffused with the sound of grunting pigs and presently he came to a sort of underground plain. To one side, a herd of giant, darkly-coloured toads were hopping along.

He looked up and could see no ceiling above, but instead an atmosphere thick with hesitant light—plum-grey tints intermixed with rusty camel.

The air was hot, stultifying. His cassock clung to his sweat-drenched body.

Going forward his feet trod over patches of some sort of plant that grew from the earth, and on closer inspection the priest found them to be daffodils, or something strongly resembling them at least—rather pretty flowers whose petals were of a rich orange hue.

Presently he came to a river. He bent over and was about to take a drink—but, as thirsty as he was, thought that it might not be wise, for there were said to be waters that made one forget, not just the immediate past, but entire lives that had been led. In one area, there were large stones in the water, and stepping from one to the next he reached the other side.

Before him, at some distance, was a long and high wall. He approached, went towards a huge gateway that was constructed of some kind of stone—some ancient structure, carved with ornate designs and covered with moss and slime.

Two huge, ugly beasts were guarding the gates—massive iron doors crusted with soot and patina that might well have been forged by Hephaestus himself. One had the head of a horse and large eyes mounted by bushy eyebrows, vermilion in colour, so they looked like flames. In one hand he held a leash, at the end of which was a three-headed dog, a snarling, frightening animal with glistening, ensiform teeth. It had the tail of a serpent, and manes made up of long, red worms that wriggled around vibrantly.

Next to him was another demon, who stood about twelve feet tall. He was black-complexioned and had the head of a buffalo. His eyes were bright disks the colour of turmeric powder. The nails of his hands were long and sharp like knives. In one hand he held a large battle axe that had a living snake wrapped around its handle.

They stood by a rickety looking sentinel station around which were scattered innumerable broken wine jugs. Before the station was a large bell that hung beneath a pagoda-like structure with a wooden striker. The two presented an intimidating spectacle, and Fr. Massimo could not help but feel some slight trepidation. Nonetheless, he approached, saluting with his hand and bowing his head when he came to them.

"I am Ashvashirsha," the horse-headed demon said, "and this is Goshirsha. This gate we guard."

"And through it I would like to walk if it leads to Purgatory."

"Purgatory?"

"It has been called by some a furnace of God's love."

"He is stupidly confused," said Goshirsha.

"I would like to enter," said Fr. Massimo.

"Do you have a pass?" Ashvashirsha asked. "No one goes through without permission from the Lord of the Dead."

The dog by its side pulled at its leash, one of the heads bared its teeth and snarled, abundant saliva dripping from its jowls. Its eyes looked desperate for violence. Another of the heads whined eagerly, while the third snapped its teeth and slobbered foam.

"I am allowed to come and go as I please." Fr. Massimo stated.

"I have heard that story before. Name?"

"Fr. Massimo Tetrazzini."

"You're a priest, eh?" Goshirsha snarled.

"Yes."

"Ah, want to push yourself around in the under-world too, do you?" He gripped his axe tightly and the serpent let off a smiling hiss. "These priests . . . "

"Is your visit for business or recreation?" Ashvashirsha questioned.

"Business. I have come to retrieve a certain soul."

"The usual story. It is always you priests who want special treatment, isn't it? Can't wait to come and fish about in the pits of hell as if the place belonged to you. Won't allow you up in Paradise but think down here it's a free for all."

"Check the list," the horse-headed demon said.

The buffalo-headed demon went into the senti-nel station and came out carrying a fair-sized iron-bound volume. He stepped quite near the priest and opened it.

"Fr. Massimo Tetrazzini you said, right?"

"Yes."

With clumsy fingers the demon turned the pages of the volume, which appeared to be of some sort of thick dark leather. A disappointed look came on his face.

"Well, it does indeed look as if your name has been added to the guest list, replacing that of one Idoai. So we won't be chopping you up today."

"Very kind of you."

Goshirsha frowned and gave him a menacing look.

"Just wait a moment and I'll ring for a guide," Ashvashirsha said. "We can't just let you tramp about on your own, wandering into restricted areas."

He struck the bell and, a moment later, a little demon page sprang up as if from nowhere. He had ears like a bat's and a wide mouth full of pointy white teeth.

"Little Josephus at your service!" he said.

"This fellow's got a pass," Ashvashirsha explained. "Take him wherever he wants to go as long as it isn't a permit G restricted area."

"Of course! Of course!"

Goshirsha set himself against one door of the gate and muscled it partially open, with a great screeching of iron; and Fr. Massimo followed the little demon through the opening, past the snapping of the three-headed dog and the angry glare of the buffalo-headed demon.

On the other side of the wall, the temperature was even hotter. The thick air wrapped itself around the priest's skin, pushed against his mouth and throat making breathing somewhat difficult. He felt as if he were standing at the mouth of a giant furnace.

"And where is it you *do* want to go?" Josephus asked as they made their way along.

"I need to see about a friend, Sister Justina—Sister Justina Monticelli, whose soul recently left the Earth. I want to have it restored."

"Restored?"

"I want it back."

"You want her soul back?"

"Yes."

"It is the Bureau of Transmigration and the Regulatory and Control Body of the Saved and the Damned that you need to go to then. It is not too far. Just follow me."

As they went along, they passed various beings of the underworld. Some were like bizarre crosses between pigs and giant centipedes. Others had only one leg, and strange elongated craniums that looked like nails. A peculiar woman with the head of a stork went riding by on a crocodile. Fat demons with skin thick like that of a rhinoceros came rolling along, and thin, wispy phantoms floated by, some moaning lugubriously, others whistling like the wind. A large bird glided overhead, wagging a bony tale and opening a beak lined with sharp teeth, a skull gripped in its talons, and an ugly fellow who looked something like an octopus came pushing himself alongside Fr. Massimo, seeming to ask for something until the little demon kicked him away.

They passed by a large lizard fornicating with a dog; the oblivion of old legends, choking oaths of darkness; sound of whips and smell of rotten eggs. A goat with the feet of a goose, distant roars, rats with bat-like wings. Troops of phantoms could be seen to one side and from them a polluted wind blew the smell of dung.

To the right there was a steep and seemingly endless slope covered with sharp blades of every description. Demons were pushing the dead down, and they would roll, being sliced into countless pieces as they tumbled. The cries of their torments reached Fr. Massimo's ears and he stopped and looked down on them with sorrow. There were sights of torture. Two demons were holding a man to the ground while a third was pulling his tongue out through his ear. Another man was tied to a stake and looked on as a number of tiny devils scraped the flesh from his bones with little knives—a festivity of ribbons and candy. An ugly naked creature, who had a huge chipped and dented sword in one hand, with his other pulled along a man by the hair as the latter screamed wildly for mercy. Then, off to one side, was a group of desperate, emaciated looking fellows eating thorns which pierced through their cheeks and lips so that blood ran down their chins.

"Come, come," Josephus said. "Don't mind them. A few hundred years of that and they'll get used to it."

"One can get used to anything I suppose."

"Oh, no! These are just the upper level torments. Down in Avici one will never get used to it. You wouldn't want to be spending your holiday there, I can tell you!"

They continued their way and presently passed over a bridge of massive construct, made of blocks of stone the size of houses, which led over a chasm out of which blue and yellow vapours rose. Down below another frightening spectacle met Massimo's eyes:

A decorative mass of grimaces. The damned. Some were being harried by animals, their limbs chewed at by sharp-fanged wolves and eyes pecked at by birds with iron beaks. Others were being thrust into huge ant-piles and covered with tremendous ants, bright strawberry in colour, which bit into their ankles and arms. And again there were others who, tied to stakes, were molested by giant flies which sucked the flesh from their cheeks and necks and left their larvae in the cavities thus made.

"These were people who in their lives were unkind to animals. People who beat dogs and killed animals and insects only for sport."

"And over there?" Fr. Massimo asked, pointing to the right, to a huge pit in which men rose and fell, serpents entwined about their arms, biting their necks—mouths deformed by agony—eyes arid salt pits—features stark, crude, as if they had been drawn there by a clumsy hand. On the banks of the pit were a few dried-up fig trees, their branches overhanging with some small amount of fruit, and the damned would reach for them, but the trees would quiver away from their grasp—thus teasing with a faint hope left always unfulfilled.

"Those are people who, when they inhabited Earth's surface, engaged in infernal cruelty. Now the

165

investment they made is paid back in a way they never could have foretold!"

Fr. Massimo's gaze wandered to one side, where he saw people floating about in a lake of molten metal, their bodies like glowing embers, orange, semi-transparent, the hair on their heads blackened ash, the singed feathers of a dove, gripping hands, stiff organs and splintered faces. The saddest of suffering, in dazzling colour, the smell of burnt things presiding over the air to the sound of cries so turbulent as to make those produced by earthly suffering seem like shallow acting. And, indeed, even in this frenzied and horrible state, these beings attempted to touch one another, stretching out their tortured limbs and lips, quivering in lascivious paroxysms.

"And them?"

"Those who dallied too long in noisome lust. Here, in their suffering, their lust is magnified a thousand times without the faintest hope of satisfying it."

"An exceedingly cruel punishment."

"There are over 150,000 of these hells," the demon said. "Here we have hells for everything, from gluttony to pride to false-friendship. There are special hells for cheating workers of their wages, raping women, cutting down trees without cause, and eating the food intended for orphans. It is a shame that they have not separated the administrative division from all the rest of it, as it isn't particularly jolly to trod about through all this dolour day and night, and it certainly doesn't give our clientele a good first impression. But what is a demon to do?"

166

Fr. Massimo expressed his sympathy and thought of all the bad people he had known, of Cardinal Zuccarelli and Bishop Vivan, and wondered which hell they were in, or if they had somehow miraculously and fortunately found redemption or the right to a less awful reincarnation—though he felt rather certain that their current abode was anything but heavenly, since few indeed are invited to dance in that sphere.

On the other side of the bridge a vast wasteland opened up before them, which they proceeded to cross. Evil-smelling smoke rose out of cracks in the earth. The air was remarkably heavy and Fr. Massimo's face shone red with heat and perspiration. It seemed to the priest that nothing could possibly inhabit such a region, but then, casting his eyes on the ground, he noticed countless little creatures, of the most minute size, crawling across it.

"The ground is covered in bugs," he said.

"Bugs? Why not at all. Those are your associates."

And, on closer inspection, Fr. Massimo realised that they were in fact tiny little priests, dressed in cassocks, reduced to an almost microscopic size and a truly horrible state. He was tempted to investigate the faces, to see who amongst their numbers he might know, but thought better of it.

He lifted his gaze and they continued forward. A long, skeletal horse went galloping by, its rider being nothing more than a few bones rattling atop its back. Off in the distance, to the left, a school of large fish were floating about in the air. Further on, the ground was dotted with a series of odd puddles—puddles, not of water, but of blood and bile in which clues of worms writhed. A few demons with grey skin were on their haunches amongst these, snacking on the body-parts of humans—nibbling on hearts and livers, chewing the flesh from ribs, swallowing down mouthfuls of brains. Every now and again they would dip their mouths into the puddles and drink from them.

Little Josephus and Fr. Massimo went on, and presently in the distance the priest saw something rising up—a hill or mountain of sorts—and onward they went. On getting nearer, however, he realised that it was a huge structure built on a variety of island in the midst of a gaping chasm—a place of grand and unique architecture, a thing that must have been built in remote times by beings of vast knowledge and strength. Narrow bridges led across the chasm into huge doors, before which extended long lines of creatures, ghosts and demons. Some stretched there necks, looking over the shoulders of those before them in the hopes of ascertaining how long the wait might be—and those towards the back of the lines stood dumbfounded, hesitant, as if uncertain whether to wait or not, their auras permeated by nervous desperation.

"Come," Little Josephus said, "I'll take you by the side entrance. Otherwise we will be waiting years to get an audience."

He led him along a very narrow edge of the ravine, where there was barely space for him to rest his feet, and then across the thinnest of bridges—a thing constructed of rope and old bits of wood which looked as if it would collapse at the slightest pressure.

Walking over it, Fr. Massimo looked down, but there was nothing but darkness as far as the eye could see. The boards creaked and cracked under his feet and flakes of wood dislodged themselves and floated into the abyss and the thing started to sway uneasily.

"Come along," the demon said. "This bridge is none too stable and I wouldn't want to have to go looking for you *down there*."

Coming to the other side, they went along the periphery of the building, traversing a thin ledge, until they came to a small wooden door, which Josephus opened and they went through, finding themselves in one of the bustling hallways of the Bureau. Little demon pages in shimmering red gowns jetted this way and that, some carrying stacks of documents or rolls of parchment, others with trays on which sat cups full of steaming liquids. A man in a great pink robe wandered forward gazing about helplessly with a confused expression on his face. A tiny little chap came running by carrying a flaming heart. Two gentlemen of important appearance whose heads were perched on immense reticella collars conversed in a corner with grave looks on their faces.

Little Josephus led Fr. Massimo up several sets of stairs, down an extensive corridor and then through a doorway on which was written "Office of the Seventh Secretary." They found themselves in a sort of anti-room at the end of which were a number of closed doors. Along one wall were ranged dilapidated benches on which mournful figures sat—a woman whose face was hidden by flowing bangs, two beaten butterfly-like wings emitting from her back; a large figure wrapped in a vast black cape, a jutting white skull extending from its folds; another man completely naked, covering his private parts with his hands; a woman whose cheeks were gouged with thick furrows made by tear flows. A few desks were there, but otherwise the only decoration was a large piece of parchment tacked to the wall on which was written:

LEAVE HOPE
AT THE DOOR

At one of the desks sat a fellow with an enormous chin, pulling vigorously on a pipe. Instead of hair growing from his head, he had weeds. A small wooden placard on the desk indicated his name to be Mr. Polevik.

"We are here to see the secretary."

"Do you have an appointment?"

"No, but this is a special case. He's on the list."

A stream of yellowish smoke floated out of the man's mouth. "Well, if he's on the list, that's another matter. Different protocol. If you two will just be seated, I'll return in a moment."

So saying, he rose from his desk and with a somewhat stiff gait made his way through one of the doors (one with the name "Mr. Rodriguez" written on it in bold lettering) revealing a large spiked tail as he went.

Josephus and Fr. Massimo sat down on a bench next to a forlorn-looking figure—a bent over fellow with a long and narrow beard that stretched to the floor.

"Are you here for your permit also?" the man asked.

Fr. Massimo replied in the negative.

"I've been waiting here for around three years. I had an appointment—but you know how these things go—bureaucracy!"

"If I might ask, what sort of a permit are you trying to obtain?"

"A home visit permit. I left a few things undone before I was pulled down here and would like nothing more than a day or two to put them in order. I went to the Office of Transmigratory Affairs and they put me on Stamp 7 status and sent me to the Department of the Deputy First Minister who said I had it all wrong and sent me to the Travel Service Security Bureau where I waited in line for about five months before being told to come here."

"I hope that they do not leave you waiting much longer," Fr. Massimo said.

"Oh, you know how it is. Without special connections it's hard to get anything done."

A minute or two later Mr. Polevik came out and said that they, Fr. Massimo and Josephus, might enter.

The two rose from the bench at which they were seated and passed in front of the line of those who had come before them and heard a distinct grumbling.

"Favouritism."

"Hand it to the priests."

"These altar boys . . ."

The room they entered was low-ceilinged, claustrophobic, but by no means small. To the front, a small bald man sat at a desk piled high with papers, folders, books of every description, abacuses, pens and bottles of ink. Behind him were ranged seemingly infinite lengths of shelves filled with giant leather-bound volumes. Numerous charts were pinned to the walls which themselves were lined with monstrous filing cabinets, the drawers of which were as large as coffins, and, between and around these, documents were stacked into towers that leaned this way and that, seemingly about to topple over in an avalanche.

The man looked up from some papers and squinted his eyes.

"I have been told that you are on the list and have some matter that you would like to bring before my attention."

"Yes, my name is Fr. Massimo Tetrazzini. I have come here regarding Sister Justina Monticelli, whose soul I believe has been brought to your world within the last twenty-four hours."

"Let us look at the recent case log."

He dug under a pile of documents and pulled out a tremendous ledger which he opened and began to scan over pages filled with minute handwriting.

"Sister Justina, Sister Justina Monticelli," he said, gazing over the pages. "Montez—Montgomery—Monticelli. Yes, yes. We have her here. A new arrival, but she's being processed on the double-quick as she's on special status. Nothing to worry about. Everything seems to be in perfect order. She'll be transmigrating shortly. Just a quick essay through the Bardo and then on she goes."

"I think not."

"Excuse me?"

"I would request her back."

The man cocked his head to one side and blinked.

"I am afraid that is out of the question," he said. "Such a thing is completely outside regulations, as is clearly stated in Directive 1,987,871,091."

"But her life was taken from her before the proper time."

"Explain."

"It was taken from her by magical means—a magic I am quite certain is being used without any sort of license or authorisation—for surely anyone who wants can't go around taking souls from their bodies and casting them about as they see fit. If rule and power were to be given to every earthly magician then before we know it the light of the moon will be considered brighter than that of the sun. Infinite justice must be founded on perfect propriety. After all, the destiny of our souls and the manner and time at which they are taken from our mortal bodies should be based on the laws of God and nature."

"It should and it is, I can quite assure you—in a manner it is!"

"Then you are assuring me that my case is a strong one."

Mr. Rodriguez showed a sour smile.

"A strong or a weak one, I am neither Lord High Chancellor of Dense Darkness nor Judge Universal," he said. "Sometimes it seems that men would be better if left unborn, for it is nothing but complaints we get once we let them out of the womb. An eternal parade of niggling awaits me outside my door. Everyone has their story. No one is satisfied with how things are run! No one comes to me and says, 'Mr. Rodriguez, I just wanted to tell you what a wonderful job you and your associates have been doing. Good work! Good work!' No—it is nothing but a splash of petty problems!"

"But about Sister Justina's case."

"Yes."

"Her soul was detached from her body."

"Yes."

"Outside of the will of Heaven."

"It is rather doubtful."

"But not impossible?"

The Seventh Secretary paused for a moment before replying in the negative.

"So you confirm that there are indeed rules for such things?" Fr. Massimo said.

"Well, naturally. There are many categories of rules and there are conditions and prerequisites for both temporary and permanent resident status in hell, reincarnation, and ascension to the various heavens. The transitional rules of the movement of souls from, to, and between the world of men and beasts and the other spheres and terraces are of course strictly regulated. Rules however are not always obeyed and the law is but imperfect."

"But surely there must be some way to sort mistakes of this nature out?"

"Well, we do of course maintain an active examination program for those who feel compelled to question our authority. If you believe there is a mistake, you will have to take it up with the Commission."

"And how long would that take?"

"Usually such cases are considered to be of low to medium priority and take around 15,000 years. By that time, of course, she would have most likely led a good many lives and the outcome of the Commission's findings would only be useful as a matter of public record. But to some people such things are important, so it is not for me to dissuade you."

"This will not do," the Italian said with irritation.

"I do not make the rules, but simply aid in their administration."

Just then there was a brisk knock on the door and it opened. Mr. Polevik stuck his head in.

"Mr. Rodriguez—the governor wants you in office 45!"

"Can't it wait? I am engaged in a case."

"He seems in a rotten mood—if I were you I would get down there without delay! You know Morax—he doesn't much care to be kept waiting."

Mr. Rodriguez scowled, and then said to Fr. Massimo: "Would you mind waiting a few moments while I deal with the matter? I shan't be long—but one must keep the caporals happy!"

The priest said that he did not mind waiting and the other left, mumbling some slight curses as he did so.

"It seems I have come here to no purpose," Fr. Massimo said.

Little Josephus, who had until then remained silent, now spoke:

"You are going about it the wrong way. In this world, as in all others, you never get something for nothing."

"But what do I have to give?"

"That I do not know. You have to find a way to alter Mr. Rodriguez' behaviour. Generally speaking, however, in this world of functionarism, the most common methods are bribery and threats. If you go by the orthodox methods, you will end up like one of those folks outside the door on the benches."

Fr. Massimo stood silent for some moments, gazing about him at all the stacks of papers. He wandered over to the desk. The ledger sat open before him. He looked down at it, saw written the name of Sister Justina Monticelli, and then recalled the words that Paul the Apostle, or at least Tychicus, wrote to the Colossians:

> *And you, being dead in your sins and the uncircumcision of your flesh, hath he quickened together with him, having forgiven you all trespasses;*
>
> *Blotting out the handwriting of ordinances that was against us, which was contrary to us, and took it out of the way, nailing it to his cross . . .*

A faint smile played on the priest's lips.

"I wonder," he said.

176

"What do you wonder?"

"What is the greatest fault in a bureaucrat?"

"There are so many, it is hard to pick out just one!"

"The greatest fault, my dear Josephus, is incompetence."

"And?"

"Stand by the door—if Mr. Rodriguez begins to open it, cough—loudly!"

He stepped back amongst the shelves, stalking along the rows of giant leather-bound volumes. They seemed to go on forever, and it was only after walking a fair distance that he found himself amongst those volumes marked 'G'—and even amongst these there seemed to be several thousand. After inspecting the spines, he finally found what he considered to be the appropriate volume on the lowest shelf. Extracting it, he noticed that it was much heavier than he would have thought, and with considerable difficulty managed to walk with it back to the desk where he set it down. Towards the back of the volume he found a page with the name Gwanru scribbled near the top of it. Below this was written:

Status: bloccato come convenuto dall'autorità tirannica della Corte Decima[†]

He took a pen from the desk and quickly added an "S" before the word "bloccato" so it read:

[†] *Status: No Admittance as judged by the tyrannical authority of the Tenth Court*

He blew on the ink until it was dry and then stuck the book back on the shelf where he had found it and returned to the front of the room and, a moment later, Mr. Rodriguez returned.

"That Morax is a real monster," he said. "The slightest trifle and he is up in arms. Sometimes he really does treat me poorly—poorly indeed!"

"No one likes a boss," Little Josephus commented.

Mr. Rodriguez gave him a dirty look and pushed by him rudely.

"Which brings us back to Sister Justina," Fr. Massimo said.

"What course do you wish to pursue?"

"That is just the question I would like to ask you. After all, your office was at fault in the case."

"My office is never at fault."

"This, Sir, is an untruth."

"It is not!"

"It is. For, aside from this case, I know full well of another in which you have blundered, though in the opposite direction."

Mr. Rodriguez' face turned bright red.

"You are beginning to bother me."

"Well, if I were to go and speak with Mr. Morax, and tell him of the foul ups going on around here, I am sure you'd be bothered a lot more. Maybe he'd ship

[†] *Status: admittance granted by the tyrannical authority of the Tenth Court*

you off to Avici, that lowest and hottest place in the universe, to shovel about in the broiling crowds."

"Are you menacing me?"

"Rather."

"What is this so called blunder of which you speak?"

"I shall not tell you. If, as you claim, one must go to the higher courts for all things, then that is where I shall go!"

"But . . ."

"But?"

"Let us reason. If you are right, which I am sure you are not. Well—if you are right, we might work out some slight bargain."

"I'd hope the bargain would not be too slight."

"You do not know me. You really do not know me."

"Sister Justina—I must have her soul back."

"What a difficult man you are," Mr. Rodriguez said, throwing up his arms. "Sister Justina, Sister Justina—there is nothing on your lips but this name. Now, out with it—tell me about this so-called blunder with which you threaten me."

"There is a certain being, by the name of Gwanru, who is currently roaming about the forests as a hungry demon, but I have it on good authority—very good authority indeed—that he should be instead in other regions."

"This I know nothing about."

"But if you would be so good as to look into the matter."

"Yes, yes, let us look."

He went back amongst the massive books and, with great alacrity, dug out the necessary volume, which he lugged back to his desk. Flipping through the pages, he came to the name in question. His eyebrows dug in towards the ridge of his nose.

"Well, well, there does seem to be some error here. A minor oversight. I have only been in this position for about six hundred years. Before that I worked at the Organised Central Bureau. My predecessor, a none-too bright fellow by the name of Dantalion, must have made the mistake."

"Undoubtedly."

"But yes—a little error," the Seventh Secretary said briskly. "Thank you. Thank you for bringing it to my attention. I will take the situation under my personal care and have it remedied. Disorder is one thing I cannot abide in the records!"

"And Sister Justina?"

"Sister Justina you say?"

"Your promise!"

"Have I promised something?"

"I was under the impression that you would return her soul."

"Return her soul?" Mr. Rodriguez laughed. "But that is impossible! Even if I wanted to, I couldn't."

Little Josephus, off to the side, let out a comical whistle.

"You will do something," Fr. Massimo stated. "I have not come all the way down to the pits of hell to play games of semantics. We had, what I believed to have been, a bargain."

180

"Calm yourself my dear Sir, calm yourself. Yes, I will do something for you. I will do something most certainly. Look, how about——"

He let his words fall and a strained expression appeared on his face. He cocked his head back and forth.

"How about what?" Fr Massimo asked.

"How about we meet in the middle. I will give you half back."

"Half?"

"Half her soul. That is the best I can offer. She has already been assigned for reincarnation, and if I gave you the whole soul back, it would put me in an embarrassing deficit. One can never be sure when one's books will be audited. If I give you half on the other hand, I can still assign the other half to the proper designee and everything will be ship-shape."

"This is absurd! That such a thing could be treated in an emporeutic fashion is astounding indeed!"

Josephus was pulling at his cassock. The priest bent down.

"You might want to take his offer," the little demon whispered in his ear. "That you have got that much of a concession is no small feat! I very much doubt that you will get more than this—and, if you press, you might get even less."

Fr. Massimo straightened himself and stood thoughtful for a moment. It seemed as if he had no choice but to accept the offer made to him.

Mr. Rodriguez gave him a questioning look accompanied by an unpleasant grin.

"So we have come to an agreement?"

The priest nodded his head in the affirmative and the bureaucrat scribbled a note on a piece of paper and then, handing it to Little Josephus, said:

"Run this down to Mr. Shen's office on Basement Level 3."

The little demon took the note, went out and, in a remarkably short period of time, returned.

"It's being taken care of," he said.

Fr. Massimo wondered where these souls in transit were kept and then considered that, if a soul might be divided in two, it must by necessity have some sort of materiality. It also would mean that the path to salvation was rather more complicated than many supposed and that Origen was, in some ways at least, correct, as were the Pharisees.

Presently the door slowly swung open. A figure stepped in—a wraith wrapped up in a great black mantle. Its mouth was nothing but a round, black hole and from it came a faint, almost inaudible rustling sound. In one outstretched hand—a hand that was nothing but a few twisted strands of bone—a package hung by a string.

Mr. Rodriguez took the package, undid the string and wrapping, and held up the phial that was within.

"Here it is."

Fr. Massimo gazed at the phial. A small strip of paper was pasted over one part with a series of numerals and letters written on it in minute handwriting. Straining his eyes, the priest could see within the glass tube a tiny white ball, not much bigger than a grain of sand. Mr. Rodriguez shoved aside some documents on his desk, and then unstoppered the phial and carefully rolled the little ball out onto the cleared space. The object quivered, vibrated slightly, letting off an almost imperceptible glow. Mr. Rodriguez opened a drawer on his desk and took out a small penknife. He put the blade to the tiny ball and, gazing close for the utmost precision, pressed down on the top of the blade with his hand, severing the thing into two almost microscopic pieces.

Fr. Massimo felt a shiver course through his body.

The Seventh Secretary, using the edge of a sheet of paper as a tool, scooted one half of the object onto the blade of the knife and replaced it in the phial, then took the other half and put it an small yellow envelope, which he sealed and then wrote the following words on:

RETURN TO ORIGINAL DESIGNEE
CASE 89UHJ897BHA21TP97845Y998305732

He rewrapped the phial and handed the package to the wraith, who took up the object and, after offering a silent bow, exited the place.

Fr. Massimo reached for the envelope.

"I will take it back with me," he said.

"Oh no, I could not entrust it to you—such a thing is absolutely forbidden," Mr. Rodriguez replied. "We have our own agents for these matters. Allow the professionals to do their jobs! Now, if you don't mind, I have a great deal of paperwork to do. . . . If, on your way out, you would just inform Mr. Polevik that he is wanted, our dealings will be at an end."

"I am counting on you," Fr. Massimo said and then with Little Josephus left the room. After advising Mr. Polevik that he was being called for, they made their way down the stairways and through the corridors and out the side door and across the fragile bridge—and then onward, back the way that they had come, until they finally stood before the great iron doors. Little Josephus banged on one and shouted for it to be opened and the massive thing screamed on its hinges.

"Be careful on the surface," the demon advised the priest as they parted ways, "I hear that it is often worse up there than down here! And do not hesitate to seek me out if you ever again need a demon of skill."

20

WHEN FR. MASSIMO returned to the village he found the people elated. To the amazement of the Patntrms, Sister Justina had revived and now sat outside on a bench in the sun, her features pale. A woman was giving her a bowl of buffalo milk to drink.

A weak smile came to her lips when she saw the priest.

"You are alive," he said.

"Yes."

"How do you feel?"

"Empty."

"I did as best I could."

"Yes?"

"Tell me what you would like."

"There is something hidden that I wish I could see. I was enveloped in mist and flashing lights. You were there too, vaguely." A troubled expression clouded her features. "Something is hidden—but whether it is gladness or sadness I cannot tell. I feel my mind. Is it also my spirit I feel? Is it also my soul? Where then is the Holy Ghost?"

Fr. Massimo was about to open his mouth, but refrained. He took her hand and held it in his, then let it go. He went back to the little church and knelt before the cross. He prayed to God.

"Lord, I am a wayfarer, but let me not be lost. I am but a vessel, O Lord, but let me not be broken. You Perpetual Presence, do not turn away. Do not turn your face away from me. Protect me from peril. Deus ad liberandum me; domine in auxilium meum festina. Tuum brachium potens est et cum volueris omnia tibi subsunt."

And then he rose to his feet.

"It is time" he said, "that I put an end to the creature that is destroying this village and causing misery to so many."

He knew well the ways of things magic, from sources both printed and unprinted, from the minor rituals to the major. He had gleaned the secrets of the Apocalypse of both heights and depths, of the twenty-two sounds and the Three Mothers. He had, through cunning and occult practices, achieved the position of Earthly Pastor of the Universal Church and, after a great fall, had managed to live on, in a new and powerful form. From Po, Kembrur and Idoai he had accrued more power. Surely whatever it was that was harassing the village he should be able to overcome? And if not—well, he was certainly ready to give up his physical form, that bag of bones he carried around, in the attempt.

He anointed his hands and body with oil of St. John's wort; took fresh borage from the garden, and pressed the juice from the leaves. He then burnt the leaves, took the ashes and mixed this with the juice. With this material he drew a crux ansata, an ankh, on his chest—that great talisman that the Angel of the Resurrection did carry in its grasp.

How would he find the culprit? The only way was to wait and watch. Sometimes one must stay still in order to advance, and patience can be the sharpest weapon.

For four nights the priest forwent sleep and took his rest during the day, reversing the habits of day and night, sitting with the upper part of his body bare, subject to vespertine chills and predawn dew. He listened; he observed; he meditated.

Sometimes he felt discouraged; sometimes elated; sometimes his spirit felt weak, for only the house of fools is the house of mirth, and though a man might feel himself to be a great thing, endowed as he is with senses, cogitation, the power to love and hate, a hungry lion will look on him as nothing more than a meal.

The fifth night came. He did as he had done on the previous nights. It was profoundly dark. A few stars twinkled small and close and seemed as if they might be picked if he were to just reach out his hand.

On the porch of the church, Fr. Massimo sat cross-legged in the darkness, his eyes open, expectant; aware, senses heightened; like a flag that picks up the slightest current of air; mind pointed towards a settled state; huge fish swim quietly in a lake; a connatural esplanade which borders the prison of chaos.

Many thoughts came to him. He considered Sister Justina. Since his return from the underworld, she had not been the same. It might be that half a soul was not better than none; and he questioned if he had made the proper choice. But it was too late to be undone. The mysteries of the universe were vast. Could he ever understand even a fraction of them?

He lifted his hand to his face and touched it. His body was indeed like clay, some well-fired porcelain—durable, but fragile nonetheless—since elephants, tigers and whales even were but temporal entities subject to the whims of nature and chance, how should he expect himself, a debile man, to traverse the world unscathed? Some antemundane impulse had brought him to this place, this state in which he was, seeming to hover between fire and aether, knowledge struggling to incubate truth within him.

Motionless he sat and watched the night. The hours dragged, one over the next, and he reasoned that this too would be a night passed without incident.

There was a faint sound in the air, like that of wind, but all was quite still. Then some squeak. A chant, like that of a distant falcon. A flicker of light passed through the plaza—a thing like a firefly—a tiny pink flame.

The priest rose to his feet and watched that light move, dance uneasily along.

It went to the hut of Cecerei, the wife of Saá, who had been slain in the Awi village, slipping under the loosely fitted bamboo door.

188

Fr. Massimo stood still for a moment and then went to the hut. Gently he pushed open the door and peered within.

The woman lay on her bed, deep in sleep, and a being was there, crouched on her blanket-covered feet; a tiny pink thing, like a wisp of coloured smoke, that had the vague appearance of a deer. It grabbed at the blanket, slowly pulling it away, and then crawled forward, along one of Cecerei's legs, in some strange, lecherous manner, and then lurched about her lush thighs and private areas. The woman's face contorted. The creature advanced over her belly, lingered around her breasts, then, passing along her throat and climbing over her chin, proceeded to press itself close against her parting lips, to cover them with its filmy form. It pulsated there, and a faint sucking sound began to emanate from it, as if it was in this manner attempting to extract Cecerei's life force.

Her right hand began to shake; her legs to agitate.

Fr. Massimo stepped forward and made himself known as, in one fluid motion of approach and attack, he swatted at the thing with his hand, catching at it with the tips of his fingers, and it felt to him like he had run them over ice.

The spectre moved from Cecerei's face to the top of her head, seeming to partially melt into her hair.

"Strange creature—enemy—hear my orders and leave this woman alone!" Fr. Massimo said in a commanding tone. "She is in my care, and you have no power over her! Take your snares away and be gone, in the names of the potent, in the names of Ruach

HaKodesh ka'sher dibber, Ruach Olam, Ruach Adonai, Ruach HaEmet, Ruach Elohim Chayim, Ruach Ha-Chokhmah, Ruach Yeshua, Ruach Yeshua Meshicheinu, Ruach Ha-Mashiach, Ruach Ha-Kodesh, Ruach Elohim, Ruach he-Chazon! Help us Sansenoi, Senoi and Sanmangelof! In the name of the great hill-shakers and those who whip up the sea—in the name of those great beings who kick over clouds and who, when quarrelling with infinite space, come out ahead, I order you to depart! Obey—obey this servant of the God of gods and detach yourself from this woman!"

The power of speech, the power of sound, is one of the greatest in the universe. Thus it is that, in the First Book of Moses, speech is placed before day and night, before sky and water, and in it God's voice is the cause of land, of grass, of seed. Syllables, it has been said, hold within them all mystical power, from that of creation to cessation—a newborn baby cries, a shout dispels an incubus—a single word joins two in an embrace of convulsive passion; a single phrase causes a war in which thousands or even millions are killed.

The creature, exposed to these syllables ripe with vigour, was as if charged with electricity—seemed to be forced away. It fell to the floor and rolled across it, flung itself into a corner and let off a shrill voice of gibberish before it became quiescent.

For several minutes the priest stood staring at it. He heard the woman groan. She sat up.

"What is it?" she asked.

"Nothing. Be still."

"Am I asleep?"

At the sound of these voices, the apparition slipped through the wall and was gone.

Fr. Massimo, without explanation to Cecerei, hastily exited the hut and caught sight of the flicker of light moving in a northerly direction. Without hesitation, he ran after it; followed it as it bounced through the forest at great speed. Fortunately, he had the power of fast walking, for a normal man, even the greatest of sprinters or long distance runners, could never have kept up with it—that thing unencumbered by physical weight—a splash of bitter milk, a squirt of black magic. And, due to the special night vision he had acquired from Idoai's bright red pit, he was able to place his steps correctly, without tripping, falling, or stumbling.

They sped over rocks and down into little valleys and then up the mountain. He did not call after it and stayed far enough back that he believed the thing was unaware that it was being chased. Down Bad Mountain they went, past the cave and the bones of Idoai now half-stripped of flesh, then to lower elevations, the creature slipping through the complex network of trees, Fr. Massimo in silent pursuit; blur of coal crossed with grey moss, wink of pearls and mist of lead; the priest feeling a strange excitement—that of the hunter forgetful of danger even as it approaches the den of the bear, approaches the place of fray.

Presently, they came to the Awi village.

"The evil has been so near all this time," Fr. Massimo thought as he caught sight of the apparition entering the back of the largest clan house, sliding through a gap in the wall.

The priest hesitated a moment, and then stepped up to the wall and peered through a crack. It was a room set aside from the rest of the house by a barrier. A smouldering fire was in the middle of the space, coals glowing. Inside a form sat in the semi-darkness—the form of Roy Tombuku, but without a mask—his identity apparent due to his physical frame, due to the sash across his chest and scar in the shape of the Mons Star on his left breast, due to the knife by his side with electric plugs hanging from its hilt. His features, seen for the first time by Fr. Massimo, were surprisingly Anglo-Saxon. His cheeks were dotted with freckles—his mouth somewhat pinched. He looked like some fretful member of the English parliament—dull, malicious eyes, lids half closed, a mouth haughty and sensual, a weak chin crusted with salt and pepper whiskers.

The creature slid about on the floor, touched the headman's feet, climbed up his body, and entered his nose. Roy Tombuku's head jerked about. His lips began to twitch and his hands started to move, making all sorts of odd gestures. He let out a deep sigh; his body shivered; and then he rose to his feet.

"An unlucky foray," he murmured and then began to scratch his lean body vigorously.

He bent down and took up his mask and placed it over his face, took up the old colonel's cap and placed it on his head; then grabbed the knife, hung the blade from the bottom of his sash and strode outside the room. A minute or so later Fr. Massimo heard a sound at the front of the building. Walking carefully around, he saw Roy Tombuku there, outside, stretching his limbs.

Dawn was not far off. The sky had turned the colour of a camel; silhouettes of hills and clouds. A parroquet cried.

The headman wandered away from the village, into the forest, and proceeded to urinate.

Fr. Massimo stepped up behind him.

"Roy Tombuku," he said.

The headman turned.

"Roy Tombuku, your evils must stop."

"Ah, it's you again! Have you come to give me your heart and head?"

"No. I have come for the very opposite reason."

"Opposite?"

"Yes."

"To do combat with the great-great grandson of Gakobus Wenge?"

"To extinguish you."

Roy Tombuku chuckled.

"Another priest like you caused me problems," he said, "and his brains I ate. But they had no tonic properties—no more than the flesh of a bird." Then, to Fr. Massimo's surprise, the other began to speak in a sort of stripped English mixed with Papuan words. "My father, Roy Henry, who came from the sky, who came with bushy skin, said that one day you would bring your life to me. He had fed 200,000 of you to the Queen and received power from the juices of countless more. My mother gave him her heart and he gave me his. Only Gakobus may suck the blood from my heart. You wish to capture me? To eat me? But you have no strong magic!"

Then thrusting himself towards the earth he began to writhe and squirm away, his skin having become glossy and flexible. He wriggled off into the trees at a surprising velocity. Some invertebrate trickery, some rank worm.

There is an art to debasement which, when brought to the extreme, becomes a mystical science. The poetry of mouldy feces and the rustling song of the weevil, while filling most with dread, are by others taken as the essence of existence. For the petroleum fly, a tar pit is the font of joy absolute. Roy Tombuku, headman of the Awi, out of reach of civilisation, out of reach of courts and judges, was able to practice his magic without fear of censure and was able see the fruits of his efforts ripen to the point of rottenness. The happiness of the maggot cannot be the same as that of the finch.

Fr. Massimo leapt after him, trying to get him beneath his boots with every step, but like a quick-moving, shuffling centipede, the other always escaped; bellying beneath foliage; slick spine turning around trees; the unpleasant face turning and grinning, wrinkling its nose, batting its eyelids.

Fr. Massimo stepped back as the other rose up in a forward motion, spinning his hand toward the priest's face.

194

When evil becomes something that does not merely exist, but is actually cultivated, it is a force of extreme power. The course of history was changed more by the tortures of Tomás de Torquemada than by the blessings of St. Francis of Assisi; the Pharaohs, by whipping men and shackling them, made the pyramids; it took no less of a hand than that of God to cleanse the Earth of the evil sorcerers, but then they sprang up again, like mushrooms, grew like the rust on iron left in the rain.

A feeling of hectic confusion burst out in Fr. Massimo's head. Thoughts shattered, white, fidgeting and reaching out for his tongue and hands and for a moment it seemed as if his mind had turned to some kind of thick fruit juice—a syrupy confused slurry of incoherent vivisection.

Roy Tombuku thrust himself at the Italian and before the latter could retreat, had him between his hands, the fingers of which had grown to some strange length. The priest dived through cogitation, attempted to pull away, but the other's grip was incredibly strong.

"By the Queen, I'm going to suck the blood from your body!" the creature said.

Fr. Massimo tried to move his arms, but they were as if frozen. He wiggled his body—but it was as if he were bound in heavy chains and he felt that surely his life was about to come to an end. He opened his lips, tried to suck air into his lungs, but found that it would not come and vaguely realised that he was beginning to collapse in on himself, felt himself retracting as if he were some snail shrinking away.

195

His own magic, his transference of consciousness, occurred to him in a vague way—but to do so he would need another being, another body—and his thoughts refused to fix themselves on any one point, refused to align themselves into a coherent pattern, moving about sluggishly like marsh water stirred by the tail of a fish.

"Leave him be."

There was a voice, an abyssal sound of red.

"Leave him be," it growled.

Roy Tombuku turned. Fr. Massimo's eyes looked, mind awoke.

A creature with long arms, chiselled body, mouth a bloody gash, came pushing itself through the trees. It was Gwanru.

"I was summoned to the underworld," he said, "but on my way, I heard you, I sensed you, like a bat senses some delicate insect, and came. I owe you a debt of gratitude."

"And what type of mud is this?" Roy Tombuku said, slackening his grip on Fr. Massimo.

"My friend," the priest murmured.

"Then he is my enemy," Roy Tombuku said, letting go of the priest. "I will dine well today."

Though Gwanru could not understand his words, he understood their purport. He opened his mouth and his jaws extended so they looked like those of an alligator. Charging forward like a ferocious lion, he snapped his teeth. Roy Tombuku stepped back, wiggled his body about and took up his blade. Then, ducking, he lunged forward, stabbing viciously at Gwanru's abdomen—but the demon managed to avoid the blade and get in a powerful facer. Roy Tombuku sprang back and stood, his legs looking like those of a greyhound. His eyes darted from right to left as he swayed his body, giving feinting impressions. He waved the knife about and the chords which were attached to its hilt shook wildly.

Gwanru advanced and Roy Tombuku moved back. The former's arms were long, and with the open palm of his right hand, struck the latter in the face, dislodging the mask, which fell to the ground.

The headman of the Awi gave a sour grin, then somersaulted forward and to the left. The knife sang through the air. Roy Tombuku pushed the blade into Gwanru's side and the latter lurched backward and then there was a quivering haze and in his place stood a young woman of striking beauty, bare-breasted, who smiled a sea of hibiscus and ivory, flashed lustful eyes at Roy Tombuku.

To say this woman was beautiful would do her an injustice—for beauty is a thing that can be appraised with calm scrutiny. But the attractive qualities of this female were not those that one could reason about or assess. They were the kind that instantly intoxicate, that drive all other thoughts from a man's head, were like nets and snares of pearls and platinum which dazzle as they entrap.

Roy Tombuku's gaze flashed over her form. His mouth opened. The cobra, hearing the sound of the pungi, freezes; the boa-constrictor, denied moisture, falls into a state of abject torpor.

It is said that trance is when the mind is singly fixed on an object and cannot be distracted by anything else. All people have their dispositions. Men are often inclined toward salacity. Roy Tombuku certainly was. The attractions of a woman would undoubtedly draw his interest. The attractions of a voluptuous nymph would hold them steadfast. The headman of the Awi was in such a trance. His eyes were open, but he was as if thrown into a dream.

This female form advanced towards him, but he did not retreat. She extended her dainty hands and caressed his face and ran her fingers over his neck and shoulders. He grinned and her nails were sharp and the back of her hands were covered with thick hair and there was no female form, no enticing beauty, no cherry blossoms or chrysanthemums and Gwanru dug his claws into Roy Tombuku's ribs. There was a cracking sound, and the face of the Awi became something awful to look at—with bulging eyes, taut lips, flaring nostrils.

Roy Tombuku whipped his arms about as a crushed mosquito might its wings.

"Be careful, his spirit will escape through his nose!" Fr. Massimo shouted.

Gwanru grabbed the other's nose and twisted it shut—shoved the head back and broke his neck. A shiver ran through Roy Tombuku's body before it went limp. He was dead.

Gwanru was breathing heavily. The knife was still stuck in his side and he was bleeding.

"I must go now," he said.

"You are hurt."

"No."

"Yes."

"It is not blades and tools that can exterminate me. I received a summons. From the underworld. I shall go and all will be well. It seems that your promise was kept."

"May you join your ancestors."

Then the demon nodded his head, rolled his eyes and turned, proceeded away, through the forest—towards the mountain—in the direction of the cave.

Fr. Massimo stood staring at the body of Roy Tombuku—a body now without power or menace. There was a stone lying nearby. He could pick it up, crack open the skull of the other, and take his red pit.

"But this magic—it is not all clean. To become infused with black magic—this should not be my ambition. If a whirlwind comes from the south, it is fair weather that comes from the north; and a fellow must be wise."

He turned and walked away, returned swiftly to Patntrm Village.

Morning was just stretching its limbs, and only a few were awake. A dog wandered up to him. He petted the animal and it licked his hand. His gaze turned towards Sister Justina's hut. She was alive, yes. But what would her life be like with but half a soul?

21

WHEN the Up-Rivers descended on the Water Bird People, it was Dom Ramiro who proved himself to be the most eager. With a stone-headed axe in his hand, he flew about, lodging it in one person after the next—attacking those mild folks who knew nothing of how to fight or wage war—who hardly even bothered to defend themselves. One swung a stick about. A few waded off into the water, tried to escape, but were caught. Most simply looked on sadly as they were chopped and broken.

The Up-Rivers wiped out the tribe, made them extinct. So it seems that those who struggle most for existence survive. Is it then any wonder that, while the average lifespan of man increases, the human heart could hardly be said to have progressed? The quiet creatures are silenced by the louder, the weaker consumed by the stronger. Towns are built not so much with bricks and logs, but with blood and the success of man is placed atop a mountain of bones.

For the Up-Rivers murder was a long practice. For the Portuguese it was as if a silver lid had been lifted off a tray of exquisite dainties. His tongue scrolled out and he licked at the fresh blood. His jaws snapped this way and that and his hands clasped—now at a severed head, now at some random gobbet of flesh.

He greedily dragged a corpse through the water, to a piece of dry land away from the crowd, where he might gorge himself without contest. Taking his axe, he brought it down again and again. A pool of red formed at his feet. He lapped at it—at that blood soup—that strange sarrabulho that warmed his throat and dampened his beard.

Drunk on carnage, he took the meat and ran with it, danced about in the water, gazed at the expiring light and jumped, swung himself forward. The merry taste of gravy, the fresh sweep of nature—he grabbed a tree, pushed his body against it, turned back to the corpse, threw himself on it, hacked away with the axe, found his feet, lurched forward, some intestines dangling from one hand, an arm grasped in the other.

He shuffled about in a world of carmine, of hardy flavour, sucking at some evil tit and wondering where he might exercise his crotch or who he might murder. Then he was close to the ground, smelling it, his heart aching for butchery, for massacre as he prodded about in dense shade, rolled through tar.

Dom Ramiro opened his eyes and looked about. He was in the forest. In one hand he held the joint of the last victim. Though his belly was still full, he tore at it with his teeth and made a sound like a hog. He then rose to his feet and wandered forward, vaguely believing he was heading back to the village of the

Water-Bird People. He did not know how far he had moved in the night, but the area around him was no longer paludal.

On he went, but did not see or hear any signs of men. He came to a rivulet and thrust his face into the water and drank, then rose up and drifted back the way he had come—or imagined he had come.

He loped through the bush for several hours—straight ahead, then to the right or left, then turning again and trying to retrace his steps. Soon clouds blotted out the sun. Rain began to fall. He crawled under an out-cropping of rocks and gnawed at his meat until the bone was naked and then he curled up and slept. Awaking in the night, he stared into the darkness and defecated; the rain had stopped; and he scratched his way along the forest floor until dawn found him, digging about for insects, grabbing up odd-coloured beetles and biting them in two, nibbling on worms and licking at larvae.

He was alone and shivered.

Somewhere in the back of his mind there were vague memories—of things like warmth, sanctuary, some faraway world in which the ground was made of flat stone and people slithered along in the bodies of beasts—the white spit of the sea and lavender and roses—sprinkling precious blood upon an altar—some rupturing heart that he wished to drink from, like a spring of florid liquid. Blood of a cow—or a man—some Christ whose small head was accented by a long, thin nose, face scavenged from apricot and beige.

202

He held his head, shook it, and held it again, his long nails delving into his temples.

Where was he?

He looked up at the sky and blinked. Was there curiosity of God? Unanswerable question; but there was certainly hunger. He walked and crawled, ran and sprang over bushes in spasms of energy, then threw himself exhausted on the ground, slugged about eating at dirt and weeds, rolled and slept, awoke, dug the balls of his feet into the earth and some mechanism in his knees and legs began to work.

Thinking he heard the sound of something falling, he looked up at the land that rose before him and made his way forward. The moon fluttered above, pecked at by the sharp beaks of stars. Light sprayed itself over his hands, but they were empty. He had no meat, felt sad, and struggled upward, towards the sun, which blinked and dipped away and then he heard heliacal voices again and went in that direction, hoping to eat out their hearts, for what was that doctrine of manslayers and whoremongers—what was it that was committed to his trust?

He reached the ridge of the mountain and looked down; and before him was a giant pit; a huge hole in the earth, a crater, roadways spiralling down into it; funicular lines and conveyor belts fingering out, the one carrying humans, the other ore—this latter to be crushed, milled, at an average of 240,000 tons daily, before the copper was put in a slurry and piped off to the coast, to be filtered and dried and then shipped off around the world—where it was made into wire, circuit boards, bells for giant churches, inconsequential sculptures of prominent citizens, and cathode ray tubes.

At the bottom of the crater, tunnels burrowed off miles into the earth, and in the tunnels men worked, dug deeper, going closer each day to hell, where they might be awaited with open arms, with blazing embraces—for as there are hells for all things, we must suppose there are also those for the people who dig about in the womb of the Mother of Giants, who shovel between the wide breasts of that woman whose children are raging waters and booming light.

22

BOOTS of burnt earth and hands of ancient pink. The cantina in the Company compound near the mine. Dead flies rested on the window sills. The annoying sound of a Jakarta idol group was playing in the background. The air was thick with the smell of alcohol, tobacco and men—expatriates and Indonesians—those whose lives had been ensnared—who had sacrificed much in order simply to work, to earn some insubstantial pay.

The workers spoke of their bad working conditions, then told jokes, laughed together, drinking beer and eating snacks, their eyes dressed in a distant sadness—the sadness of men forced to live without family, expending their lust on prostitutes and spending their days beneath the Earth's crust, away from the glorious sun.

One man came in, a concerned look on his face. "Did you hear?"

"What?"

"Raharjo, they found him about an hour ago."

"Found him?"

"Dead."

Everyone's eyes opened wide.

"An accident?"

"Hardly. Some animal killed him and ate away his flesh."

"Animal?" Julius Lesmana asked.

"It seems that it might have been a tiger."

"Terrible!"

"So very bad!"

"That is why these forests need to be logged out. There are too many animals."

"More hunting."

"Yes."

The conversation drifted this way and that; a few games of cards played; and Julius got up and left the place; went back to the barracks to sleep. He was thirty-two years old and held a foreman position that earned him a dollar and a half an hour; a miserable wage hardly befitting the nature of work in which he was engaged. That night he dreamed of vines.

The next morning he was driving a jeep along the access road to the Deep Ore Zone. The road was narrow. Densely-forested mountains rose up to right and left, their peaks draped in mist. He was in no rush to get to his destination, hardly feeling that his pay level was consistent with the need for alacrity, and stopped his vehicle to smoke a cigarette. He lit up and then stepped out, looking over the landscape.

The air was cool. He dragged the smoke into his lungs, vaguely appreciative of the beauty of his surroundings, but feeling a sense of exile, a fish chucked through outer space—man feeling apart from trees and plants and stones—thinking nature should be a pleasure-garden or reserved merely for bad oil paintings to be hung in geometrical houses. Receiving a weight against his back, his face was in the mud. His heart kicked at his chest. He was conscious of something gripping into his neck. Surprise and terror fought against each other as he struggled to free himself, as he felt his lifeblood gush from his neck and mix with the mud and the last thing he saw was a hairy face and red, snapping teeth.

Later, when some men from the mine found his mutilated body, lying about a hundred and fifty metres away from the jeep, it looked as if it had been fed on by wild animals.

"It is not a wild animal," a Company doctor pointed out. "Observe the teeth marks. They are of a human!"

"These damned cannibals!"

The Company had long ago attempted to resettle all the locals—had carted them off to the distant coast where they had gone hungry, died of malaria, lost their lives, using para-commandos to kill or arrest those that resisted. There was little room for West Papuans in West Papua. Years before, the World Bank had helped finance colonization, by donating large amounts of money toward bringing Javanese into the land. They further put funds into road building, so the highlands could be penetrated. They called all this "investing in the future of West Papua," and Bank officials, greedy eyes magnified by thick-lensed glasses, spoke of "infrastructure for sustainable development" and the "dreams of development." Where other men might have seen beautiful forest, these *money men* saw "timber" (We calculate the weighted average timber value of every hectare of West Papuan forest to be approximately USD 13,504. This does not include stumpage cost.) Where other men saw mountains, these *bank men* saw vaults containing gold, copper, and groaning silver. Where other men saw swamps and meadows, these men in jackets and ties saw tankers full of oil.

Indeed, men who had grown up in the cities of America, who spent their days invested in wool suits, trousers kept up with burnished calf belts, their feet encased in crocodile loafers with little tassels on them, planned out the entire future of a land that was not their own, that they did not know and at best had only seen in the most shallow manner. Every last stick and rock, every drop of water and every hope was divvied up—allotted to men who lived in Phoenix, Arizona, and New Orleans, Louisiana.

And so it is that they sit in the lurking places of the cities and towns and villages, and in secret places murder the innocent, with eyes privily set against the poor. And as a strong wind picks up dried leaves and blows them through the air, men are blown this way and that by their own greed, spinning wildly about, though to them things seem stable.

The mine security officers fanned out through the jungle. They carried rifles. Their boots crushed plant life, squashed beetles. They came to a dip in the landscape and descended, murmuring to each other what they would do to the cannibal once they caught him, their faces ugly as they spoke of torture, of various ways they might kill him—this enemy of civilisation who did not realise that eating man flesh was taboo. For one might gorge on the brains of cows, the tendons of sheep, the tonsils of egrets—one might stuff one's mouth with the intestines of bears or suck down the arms of an octopus—but dine on so much as the finger of man and you are forever banned, not simply from the beau monde, but from the human race itself.

The forest rested in silence. Only the sound of their steps. A bird flew off from a branch. A man coughed.

Then a being, completely naked, darted through the trees before them.

"That's him! Primitive bastard!"

"Catch him alive!"

"To hell with that!"

Two men raised their rifles and, almost simultaneously, fired.

Dom Ramiro felt a stinging pain in his left leg. He grabbed it, tried to run on, and fell. A bullet had ripped through his thigh, an illumination of magnificent friars and boiling wine.

What were the duties of a priest? To be above sorrow and grief and to lick at leprous scabs and to seethe in humbleness and to feel your leg on fire with impurities pouring out of it. A white collar convert nation in baptisms snapped at by lions Nossa Senhora marriages, what was he doing there, but where was it, the helicopter? In him things began to latch together, thoughts to come up from within him. Amber shapes. In the mind, in the soul. Yes. West Papua. The Pontifical Mission Guild. The Lord's work. A hunger for others. The ignorant he must convert. He saw the men approaching, pointing rifles at him. Ears and hair. Their faces were brambles of hate, nests of aggression.

His lips quivered. His tongue wagged. He waved his hand.

"I—I'm a priest," he said in Portuguese, just before four bullets finished him off.

23

WHAT imagination it took to make a world in which rain falls and then clouds are dispersed by the rays of the sun; in which wings whip the air and prostomiums stir the earth; where cygnets open their beaks and crocodiles their jaws and some heavenly beings are decked in the unpolluted radiance of gold. Where the luxuries of Heaven and the stones of the Earth are both ominous and luminous and noble ophitis respires the breath of life.

"You have no happiness," Kiafuri told Fr. Massimo.

"I am unsure."

"Your eyes are sure."

"Maybe."

"You have been here a long time. I stay because this is my place, but you?"

"To help."

"And you have. But when you feed a man, you do not look on as he digests. Why would a man want to give up his home to live in that of another? Is it then so bad where you come from? To help a neighbour and then return home is understood. To help him and then remain at his house is not."

Fr. Massimo shrugged his shoulders, turned and walked away. Sister Justina was coming towards him. They met on the path.

Her gaze was vacant.

"How do you feel?" he asked.

"Fine."

"I am glad."

They stood silent for a few moments. He looked at her round, rather plain face and then at the ground; wanted to speak, but no words came to him. There was a certain unreality to the situation—like two ghosts meeting, but not having the ability to communicate.

"I shall go and pray," she said.

"Yes."

He watched her as she made her way toward the church. Indeed, in the last days, the woman had done little else but pray. She rarely talked with anyone and, when she did, it was without animation, in a few required syllables unadorned by inflections of joy. He recalled how she had been in Florence—how she would read to him and had made him a wool cap. It was true that then she might not have been happy, but she certainly had been whole. He had, he reflected, through his own egoism, thought of himself as her benefactor.

"I am a fool," Fr. Massimo murmured to himself. "I should have never brought her here."

He wandered over to the village garden. Bees swung around zucchini blossoms. A fecund aroma came from the heated earth. He knelt and pulled some weeds from around the cucumber plants. Though he normally enjoyed working in the garden, he felt rather sad doing so that day.

"No matter how much a man can know," he thought, "his knowledge is truly small. A genius and an idiot are not so far apart as they would seem. The hare thinks itself large when it sees a shrew, but that is because it has never been in the presence of an elephant. And is it not possible for the sower to overtake the plowman?"

He grasped soil in his hands, felt tired.

There was a peach tree, a tree that his predecessor, Don Renzo Bazzoffi had planted, and he sat beneath it; leaned his back against the trunk; mind wandered; some small boy offering him a ripe peach, him taking, eating it, a flow of thick, sugary juice, a strange, intoxicating sap. When he opened his eyes someone was near him, but he was unable to see the other's face since it shone with bright light. Fr. Massimo spoke to the being and received reply about how the altar had been looked after but that it could no longer be.

"What should I do?" Fr. Massimo asked.

"Sinning angels are forever encroaching on virtue and universal omnipotence no longer wishes to raise its hand to support fleeting faith and vomiting lies. Would you not let gold plate fall so that you might grasp the diamond chalice? Is your resolution so feeble that you would wallow in the swamps of hell but not so much as glance at the shimmering clouds? Do not be tempted by holiness or truth, for once you think of truth you are far distant."

213

"Then is nothing true?"

"When Phidias made the god, it was based neither on truth or falseness."

"Then on what?"

"Well, you are not the poorest man on earth, so more should not be said."

"No?"

"No. Go out of the room, come into the room."

It was dusk when he stood up. The world around did not seem quite the same. Not that anything had materially changed. But the world's hollowness seemed to have taken on a new resonance. For how long had he slept? The burden of the valley of vision.

He looked up at the outline of the hills and felt a sudden yearning for other things, other sights, other experiences; to see men rushing about and to hear broken silences.

EDWARD HERON-ALLEN *The Complete Shorter Fiction*
EDWARD HERON-ALLEN *Three Ghost-Written Novels*
J.-K. HUYSMANS *The Crowds of Lourdes*
J.-K. HUYSMANS *Knapsacks*
COLIN INSOLE *Valerie and Other Stories*
JUSTIN ISIS *Pleasant Tales II*
JULES JANIN *The Dead Donkey and the Guillotined Woman*
GUSTAVE KAHN *The Mad King*
MARIE KRYSINSKA *The Path of Amour*
BERNARD LAZARE *The Mirror of Legends*
BERNARD LAZARE *The Torch-Bearers*
MAURICE LEVEL *The Shadow*
JEAN LORRAIN *Errant Vice*
JEAN LORRAIN *Fards and Poisons*
JEAN LORRAIN *Masks in the Tapestry*
JEAN LORRAIN *Monsieur de Bougrelon and Other Stories*
GEORGES DE LYS *An Idyll in Sodom*
GEORGES DE LYS *Penthesilea*
ARTHUR MACHEN *N*
ARTHUR MACHEN *Ornaments in Jade*
CAMILLE MAUCLAIR *The Frail Soul and Other Stories*
CATULLE MENDÈS *Bluebirds*
CATULLE MENDÈS *Mephistophela*
ÉPHRAÏM MIKHAËL *Halyartes and Other Poems in Prose*
LUIS DE MIRANDA *Who Killed the Poet?*
OCTAVE MIRBEAU *The Death of Balzac*
CHARLES MORICE *Babels, Balloons and Innocent Eyes*
GABRIEL MOUREY *Monada*
DAMIAN MURPHY *Daughters of Apostasy*
KRISTINE ONG MUSLIM *Butterfly Dream*
OSSIT *Ilse*
CHARLES NODIER *Outlaws and Sorrows*
HERSH DOVID NOMBERG *A Cheerful Soul and Other Stories*
PHILOTHÉE O'NEDDY *The Enchanted Ring*
GEORGES DE PEYREBRUNE *A Decadent Woman*
HÉLÈNE PICARD *Sabbat*
JEAN PRINTEMPS *Whimsical Tales*
RACHILDE *The Princess of Darkness*
JEREMY REED *When a Girl Loves a Girl*
ADOLPHE RETTÉ *Misty Thule*

JEAN RICHEPIN *The Bull-Man and the Grasshopper*
FREDERICK ROLFE (**Baron Corvo**) *Amico di Sandro*
JASON ROLFE *An Archive of Human Nonsense*
ARNAUD RYKNER *The Last Train*
LEOPOLD VON SACHER-MASOCH
   The Black Gondola and Other Stories
MARCEL SCHWOB *The Assassins and Other Stories*
MARCEL SCHWOB *Double Heart*
CHRISTIAN HEINRICH SPIESS *The Dwarf of Westerbourg*
BRIAN STABLEFORD (editor)
   Decadence and Symbolism: A Showcase Anthology
BRIAN STABLEFORD (editor) *The Snuggly Satyricon*
BRIAN STABLEFORD (editor) *The Snuggly Satanicon*
BRIAN STABLEFORD *Spirits of the Vasty Deep*
COUNT ERIC STENBOCK *The Shadow of Death*
COUNT ERIC STENBOCK *Studies of Death*
MONTAGUE SUMMERS *The Bride of Christ and Other Fictions*
MONTAGUE SUMMERS *Six Ghost Stories*
ALICE TÉLOT *The Inn of Tears*
GILBERT-AUGUSTIN THIERRY *The Blonde Tress and The Mask*
GILBERT-AUGUSTIN THIERRY *Reincarnation and Redemption*
DOUGLAS THOMPSON *The Fallen West*
TOADHOUSE *Gone Fishing with Samy Rosenstock*
TOADHOUSE *Living and Dying in a Mind Field*
TOADHOUSE *What Makes the Wave Break?*
LÉO TRÉZENIK *The Confession of a Madman*
LÉO TRÉZENIK *Decadent Prose Pieces*
RUGGERO VASARI *Raun*
ILARIE VORONCA *The Confession of a False Soul*
ILARIE VORONCA *The Key to Reality*
JANE DE LA VAUDÈRE *The Demi-Sexes and The Androgynes*
AUGUSTE VILLIERS DE L'ISLE-ADAM *Isis*
RENÉE VIVIEN AND HÉLÈNE DE ZUYLEN DE NYEVELT
   Faustina and Other Stories
RENÉE VIVIEN *Lilith's Legacy*
RENÉE VIVIEN *A Woman Appeared to Me*
ILARIE VORONCA *The Confession of a False Soul*
ILARIE VORONCA *The Key to Reality*
TERESA WILMS MONTT *In the Stillness of Marble*
TERESA WILMS MONTT *Sentimental Doubts*
KAREL VAN DE WOESTIJNE *The Dying Peasant*

www.ingramcontent.com/pod-product-compliance
Lightning Source LLC
Chambersburg PA
CBHW020142120726
47903CB00007B/2381